O'NEILL'S TEXAS BRIDE
By
Caroline Clemmons

O'Neill's Texas Bride

Caroline Clemmons

Copyright 2015 Caroline Clemmons

Cover Graphics
Lilburn Smith

All rights reserved. Without limiting the rights under copyright reserved above, no part of this publication may be reproduced, stored in or introduced into a retrieval system or transmitted in any form or by any means (electronic, mechanical, photocopying, recording, or otherwise) without the prior written permission of both the copyright owner and the above publisher of this book.

Names, characters, places, and incidents are either the product of the author's imagination or are used fictitiously. Any resemblance to actual persons living or dead, businesses, events, or locales is purely coincidental.

CAROLINE CLEMMONS

Dear Reader,

Thank you for choosing my book from all the millions available. I love, love, love my readers and am so appreciative of your loyalty. I write for you. If ever you have comments or suggestions, I would love to hear them at mail to: caroline@carolineclemmons.com If you want to stay current on when I release a new book, please sign up for my newsletter. I hope you enjoy this book. If you do, please leave a review when you've finished at wherever you purchased the book.

Again, thank you,

Acknowledgments

Special thanks to my wonderful husband, Hero, for his encouragement now and in the past. Also to my lovely daughters for their help and support.

What a wonderful critique group I have. I couldn't have completed this book without your encouragement and nudging/dragging me forward.

Thanks to my editor, Stephanie Suesan Smith, PhD at http://www.edit.stephaniesuesansmith.com

O'NEILL'S TEXAS BRIDE

Chapter One

September 1885
Lignite, Texas

Stella Clayton grabbed her brother's shoulders. "What's happened?"

Lance gasped out, "Cave in. I can't find Papa."

Grabbing her shawl, Stella joined her mother and sister as the women and boy ran to the mine's mouth at the base of a hill.

Other families from the small town gathered, the females standing silently while men milled around or worked to free those trapped. The shriek of a whistle and shouts of men swarming the rock strewn work area created an atmosphere like another world.

She pulled her shawl around her shoulders. "What happened? Does anyone know?"

Her brother shrugged. "When I couldn't find Papa, I asked but no one would answer me."

Grace tugged the foreman's sleeve. "What crew was caught?"

Wiping sweat and grime from his face, the foreman turned impatiently. "Calm yourself, Mrs. Clayton. Your man is helping dig through to them."

He waved abruptly at those crowded around him and spoke loudly. "Stand back and let us do our jobs."

Stella exhaled her relief and thanked God her father had been spared this time. Small groups of crying and praying women huddled as she and her mother and sister did now.

She whispered to her sister, "How many times have we stood with Mama like this?"

Brushing a stray lock of blond hair from her face, Nettie sighed. "I've lost count. I've no wish to marry a miner and live with this kind of fear every day."

"I won't marry one. I'll not sentence me or my future children to this sad life. No man but our sweet Papa is worth the worry and sacrifice.

Every day he goes into that mine is torture for Mama."

Nettie shook her head slowly. "But where will we meet such men? All we know are miners."

She met her sister's gaze. "We could teach school elsewhere. I know we could pass the exam."

Sorrow tinged blue-green eyes so like her own. "We already teach school. What will happen to our students when we go elsewhere? And what will Mama do without us?"

Stella had no answer for Nettie. She'd asked the same questions of herself many times. Convincing the mine's owner to let them set up school in a vacant building had been difficult. Even though he'd reluctantly agreed, he didn't provide any supplies except a stove and coal to heat the school in winter.

She paced in front of her mother until Mama told her to sit down. Pulling her shawl closer, she joined Mama and Nettie on the ground. Lance stood far behind them with two friends.

Behind them a few hundred yards up another rise stood rows of the clapboard houses furnished for married workers. To the right loomed the equipment to crush and convey the coal to the railroad cars. To the left were the company store and single men's dormitories, called longhouses. Nearby, a train carrying coal pulled out of Lignite headed west.

Six long hours later, four filthy men emerged from the mine. Six had been in the crew. Eager women and children crowded around the men. Behind them, the tall figure of her father bent under the weight of the limp body he carried over his shoulder. Behind him, Mr. Karpinski carried a second body. As four families rejoiced in relief, two sobbed in sorrow.

The Claytons rushed to Council Clayton as soon as he was free of his sad duty. Almost unrecognizable from the coating of black dust and grime, he led them silently home. Eager to escape the scene, they restrained their questions until out of sight of those whose men hadn't survived.

Brown, gray, and black dust covered everything this near the mine and equipment. Laundry could only be hung on the line when the breeze was from the southwest or the clean clothes became gray with soil carried in the air. Stella hated the dismal looking town.

Once in the simple frame home provided by the mine company, Papa slumped near the stove, coughing in his usual evening attempt to clear his lungs. Slowly, he rose to wash the grime from his face and hands.

Mama set the pot of stew on the table while Stella put out the bowls and spoons. Nettie fetched mugs of cider. Lance brought the bread and knife then watched as if torn by indecision.

Between bites of stew, her father looked at his wife. "Someone was careless and caused the cave in. Or, it was done deliberately. There was no structural reason for the walls to give way. I'm as sure as I know my own name."

Mama grabbed his arm. "Not an accident? Oh, Clayton, you could have been one of those trapped."

He clasped her hand and kissed her palm. "I wasn't, love. Haven't I worked coal since I was ten? I haven't reached the age of forty-five by being careless."

Stella couldn't resist another attempt to reason with her father. "We left England to start a new life, Papa. Please try to find a different line of work. Something safer."

"And cleaner." Nettie smiled and eyed their father's blond hair tinged black beneath the line that had been covered by his hat.

He met Stella's gaze and pointed his spoon at her. "Stella Grace Clayton, don't start that again. Mining is all I know and you'll say nothing else on the matter."

Papa using her full name silenced her for now, but she had no intention of giving up her quest permanently.

She hadn't meant to hurt his feelings. "I'm sorry, Papa. I meant no disrespect. You're the best father in the world and you know we love and look up to you."

He smiled at her.

Mama shushed her daughters. "Leave your father be, girls. Can't you see he's exhausted from saving lives and toiling to put this food on the table?"

Why wouldn't Papa try to find another job? His excuse of knowing only mining rang hollow in her ears. This was no way to live, risking a cave in or explosion daily. There had to be a better, safer job somewhere. He'd learned to mine, so why couldn't he learn a new trade?

She turned her attention to her brother. Lance must never give in and become a miner.

After they'd finished the meal and cleaned the kitchen, Stella spoke low to her brother. "Meet me outside by the corner of the house."

She slipped out the door and waited for Lance. When he joined her, he appeared distressed.

"What's upset you?"

Hands in his pockets, he looked at the ground. "Some of the fellows have been giving me a hard time. I'm branded lazy and a mama's boy because I don't work with Papa or anyone else."

"Tomorrow, go to the store and ask if they need help sweeping and such."

He sent her a stony glare. "I've already been there. They hired Mr. Haney because he's too injured to work in the mines since that beam fell on him two weeks ago."

She patted his shoulder. "We'll think of something else then."

His face darkened in anger. "Don't you see? I'll have to go into the mines because there's no escape for the likes of me. There *is* nothing else. We've been over this before. Soon, I have to start doing my part for the family." He strode off into the dark.

There had to be another way. In her head, she realized someone had to pick the coal from the ground because everyone needed the fuel. Yet in her heart, she refused to see her intelligent brother sacrifice his dreams to futility. What could she do to help Lance?

***

Texas Hill Country

Finn O'Neill guided the chestnut gelding around the corral, offering the animal encouraging murmurs.

He halted the animal and smoothed a hand along the neck before grabbing the pommel. "That's right, boy, you can do this. See, Dominic, I'm just swinging me leg over your back now. Steady."

Dominic swung his head, but tolerated Finn's weight added to the saddle. After three times around the ring, Finn dismounted and walked the horse into the barn for cool down and brushing before feeding him.

Smiling, Dallas McClintock, Finn's brother-in-law, strode toward them. "Great work. You have the gift, Finn. Sure glad you're here."

Finn basked in the praise, but he wanted more. "Sure and 'tis glad I am to work with a fine horse like this. He'll be as good as his father, Dominion, you mark my words."

No matter how much he appreciated all Dallas had done for the O'Neill family, Finn yearned for more. His own land. His own horses. His own home and family.

He admired and respected his brother-in-law and the fine husband he'd made for Cenora. He'd been more than kind to the O'Neill family. But living as a hanger-on didn't suit Finn.

As if reading his mind, Dallas clapped him on the shoulder. "You'll have your own place soon, or I miss my guess."

Finn looked up from brushing Dominic. "And how would I be doing that? I've no money except the wages you pay me. While you're a generous man, I'll be old as Da before I can buy me own land."

"Nonsense. You're a hard worker and resourceful." Dallas leaned against the stall. "Say, I just learned the Lippincotts are selling their ranch. He stopped by this morning to give me first refusal. Told him you'd likely be interested."

News of the availability of the fine place ignited a longing strong enough to taste. Hadn't he admired that ranch since he'd seen it? Hadn't he dreamed of owning such a place?

"And did a miracle occur that I suddenly have money? Just to torment me, tell me how much they're asking?"

Dallas named an amount. "Believe they'd come down a bit to get a good buyer they could trust to carry on as they've done. Lippincott's proud of the set up he's built and hates that his sons don't want any part of ranching."

Stepping into the shade of the screened-in back porch, the men lingered near a table that held a bucket of water. Finn filled the dipper and took a drink. He dipped the ladle into the bucket again, this time letting the cool water flow over his head, plastering his hair and drenching his shoulders.

"Though the price is reasonable, I've no way to raise that much." Knowing the perfect place was out of his reach hurt his pride. He should have spared himself frustration and not asked about the cost.

"Have you thought of asking Grandpa to back you? Or Austin? They both think a lot of you and the way you've helped Cenora and me."

As he handed the dipper to Dallas, a spark of hope exploded in Finn's chest. "I've nothing to offer as collateral against me failure, man. Why would they trust me?"

Dallas copied Finn's actions on himself then returned the dipper to the pail. "Why wouldn't they? Never know unless you ask."

"I'm only kin by marriage and they owe me nothing. I've no right to ask their generosity."

"Narrow thinking, man. If Austin hadn't helped me, I wouldn't have been able to buy this ranch from Marston. Austin and Kathryn didn't owe me wages because they raised me, but they paid me anyway.

Frankly, I always suspected Austin agreed to pay Marston if I defaulted."

Finn rubbed his jaw. "Don't know if I could ask either your grandfather or uncle for a loan, but yearning for that ranch eats at me insides. Sure and I'll think on it."

He thought of nothing else the rest of the day. A dozen reasons for and against near froze him. No more shilly shallying. If he didn't make a move, the prime ranch would be snapped up by someone else and then he'd regret not having at least tried for himself.

The next morning when he came into the kitchen for breakfast, surprise showed on his sister's face. "And what are you doing wearing your best shirt and britches this morning? You trying to impress one o' the horses?"

Dallas laughed and kissed Cenora. "Don't be giving your brother a hard time, love."

Finn sat and spread his napkin across his lap while he peered at Dallas. "With your permission, I'll be riding into town about that matter we discussed yesterday."

"Good to hear." Dallas toasted him with his coffee mug. "Slàinte."

Cenora rested her fists on her hips, a sure sign her temper had flared. "You'll not be keeping secrets from me, Dallas McClintock. What're you and me brother talking about?"

Dallas patted her protruding stomach. "Nothing to worry you, little mother. Sit down, love, and let's eat the food you've prepared. I'm famished and your biscuits are light enough to float away."

She took her seat, but glared at both men. "Flattery won't make up for shutting me out o' your secrets."

Finn set down his cup. "Don't fash yourself, sister. I'm only doing groundwork for a project I have in me head. You'll know soon as I have something to tell."

After breakfast, Finn rode into McClintock Falls. He worried about approaching Dallas's grandfather, Victor McClintock, about a loan. More, he dreaded seeing Dallas' grandmother, Zarelda. That woman must have been born sucking lemons and sour pickles.

Rarely had he seen Mrs. McClintock smile. She had no love of Dallas' mixed Cherokee blood and even less use for the Irish. If she heard his proposal, he could count on her using all her power to block the deal.

Mayhap he should skip the elder McClintock and seek out Dallas' uncle Austin and his kind wife, Kathryn. No, the older man had more money than he needed while Austin and Kathryn had a pack of kids still at home. By the time Finn reached the gates of the McClintock's long drive, his stomach was churning so he thought he'd have to dismount and throw up in the hedges.

Buck up, boyo. This is your future on the line.

At the front hitching ring, he gave his reins to the stable boy who raced toward him. After removing his hat and slicking back his hair, he straightened his shoulders. No turning back. Fear still gripped his gut but he forced himself to climb the steps and turn the bell's ringer.

He'd never begged for anything in his life. Sure, he'd watched begging members of the Irish Travelers his family had lived with for several years. But the O'Neill's didn't beg and now were finished with the traveling life.

Asking for a loan wasn't the same as begging, or so he tried to tell himself. No matter how he argued with himself, his heart told him otherwise. A real man made his own way. Only the memory of Lippincott's vast land and grand house could lower him to request help from Victor McClintock or anyone else.

A starched and proper maid answered his summons and left him cooling his heels in the foyer while she sought permission for him to be seen. While he stood like a statue, he heard the rumble of men's voices. Curse the luck. He'd counted on McClintock being alone. The maid soon returned and he followed her to the elder McClintock's study.

The man who insisted he call him Grandpa stood and gestured to a leather wing chair. "Come in, Finn, and have a seat. We were just talking about you. Wally, this is the man who might help you out."

Reclaiming his chair, McClintock said, "This is my wife's nephew, Wallace Farland. He's here seeking help for a problem."

The other man was middle aged with thinning brown hair and an elaborate mustache that curled on each end. He looked from McClintock to Finn and back. When McClintock nodded, Farland spread his hands across his paunch.

"I own the Farland Coal Mine at Lignite, Texas southwest of San Antonio. Someone is causing so-called accidents and also discord among the miners. I need a man who can be my eyes and ears."

Farland waved his hand toward Grandpa. "While I came here to ask Uncle Victor about one of his grandsons, you might fit in better. I've several Irish miners as well as other immigrants and Mexicans. Work has slowed down and I'm losing money. Something is going on and I mean to have answers."

Finn struggled to hide his instant dislike of the mine owner. "I'm a rancher, sir. Sure and I came here to ask Grandpa McClintock for a loan to buy the ranch next to that o' Dallas. We'd like to be partners in raising fine horses, you see."

Farland looked down his nose at him. "I'd pay you double if you worked for me. You could blend in, find out who's causing trouble. Then you'd be able to save toward the down payment."

Down payment? Did the man think he was daft? Didn't he know how little miners made for working long hours?

"Beggin' your pardon, Mr. Farland, but the land in question won't long be on the market. I must act today or risk losing the perfect property." Finn turned his attention to Victor McClintock.

Grandpa nodded. "I'd like to see you and Dallas in business together. I haven't forgotten you saved his life and that of my son Austin against those rustlers. And I know how hard you've worked to help Dallas build his growing reputation."

He leaned forward. "Tell you what, you help Wally and I'll advance you the cash you need."

The load of worry that weighed down Finn lightened so suddenly he felt giddy. Could he be hearing right? "I'm that grateful, Grandpa McClintock. Can we work out the terms?"

Wallace Farland pulled out his pocket watch and frowned. He replaced it in his vest. "Excuse me, Uncle Vincent, but I have to get back to Lignite." He speared Finn with a look. "You and I need to work out details before I leave."

Again, Finn schooled his features. Did the man always interrupt instead of deferring to his elders? "What would you expect o' me?"

"You'll need to dress in work clothes. You have work boots instead of those of western style?"

"Aye, I have an old pair that looks fit for the dustbin but I wear them to muck out the stalls. And I have old clothes. We throw nothing away."

"Good. You'd hire on as any other miner. Once a week, you need to walk to the next town of Spencer and mail me a letter to the name I give you and he'll send it on to me. You should tell me what you've learned."

"And do you suspect any men so far?"

"I do but I've no proof. Council Clayton, Aleski Karpinski, and Johan Swensen are under suspicion. But they may be innocent and others guilty. That's why I need a man who works with the miners every day."

"Are there lodgings nearby where I can sleep and eat?"

The mine owner puffed out his chest. "You'll stay in the single men's longhouse where you can sleep for a dollar a week. A dining room is attached and your food will be furnished at a small charge. In addition, there's a store where you can find any supplies you want."

Finn had a bad feeling about the whole set up but his desire for Lippincott's land and house overrode his misgivings. "And will I be paid in cash or scrip? When I traveled through some states, I saw miners cheated out o' what was due them by low pay in scrip and them having to use it at the company store."

Farland's face turned red. "Now see here, I'm fair to my workers. The scrip is simply a way to keep track."

He couldn't risk killing the chance to get his loan. "Sure and I meant no accusation. I only made an observation from my time passing through West Virginia."

"Harrumph. I have nothing to do with the people there. You have any other questions?"

"What if I can't find proof o' who's causing trouble?"

"Someone is guilty. I'm sure a smart man working among the miners can discover who's to blame. All you have to do is mingle with the men and keep your eyes and ears open. That shouldn't be hard, now should it?"

"No, Mr. Farland. I understand what you're asking and 'tis me best I'll do."

"Fine, fine, O'Neill, report to the mine and act as if you're any other man looking for a job. You can send me reports by mail."

Finn stood and shook the mine owner's hand. "I'll be there as soon as I can work out departure with me brother in law. He won't keep me overlong since he's that anxious for me to get the ranch next to his."

When Farland had supplied a mailing address to his contact and left, Finn resumed his place in front of McClintock's desk.

Grandpa leaned back in his chair. "That's settled, then. Now tell me about this ranch."

"Yesterday Lippincott said he's selling out and offered Dallas first refusal because the ranches adjoin. Lippincott and his wife are moving into town. His children don't want to carry on the ranch, which must be a great disappointment for the man."

Surprise spread across Grandpa's face. "Lippincott's selling?

That's news, but I know his wife's in bad health. Good set up there. What's he asking?"

Anxiety clutched at Finn's throat. 'Twas a princely sum, but 'twas a grand place. He named the price and held his breath while he waited for Grandpa's decision.

Grandpa masked his opinion, but drew a sheet of paper toward him and took up his pen. The older man pursed his lips and wrinkled his brow in concentration as he jotted figures.

Seconds seemed like hours to Finn. The mantel clock ticked away with a monotonous sound. Sweat gathered under his arms and on his brow. What would he do if Grandpa changed his mind?

"Here's what I worked out. I'll go see old Lippincott today and seal the deal. I'm sure you and my grandson can square your time off to work at the mine. You can pay me back over fifteen years."

He turned one of the pages toward Finn. "Here's what the payments will be each January. Since it's so late in the year, you won't owe a payment until 1887."

Finn gulped. "Sir…Grandpa, these are generous terms. What if I can't figure out who's causing the trouble at your nephew's mine?"

Grandpa waved away his concern. "All you can do is your best. But I reckon you'll do it, Finn. I have confidence in you."

Feeling as if his heart would burst, Finn left the McClintocks. He peered at the puffy white clouds floating in the bright blue sky overhead. Didn't he feel he was floating on one of those?

He reined the horse toward home. Not his precisely, but where he lived with his sister and brother in law. He couldn't believe his dream was within reach at last. How long before he could move into his own place?

Chapter Two

Lignite, Texas

Finn extinguished the candle on his hat as he emerged from the coal mine's inky interior with his six-man crew. They worked in a section of the mine with five other crews. Each crew raced against the others. How he hated this backbreaking job and he'd only been here a week.

He was that grateful his time here was temporary. Nothing except the Lippincott ranch dangling in front of him could persuade him to continue. A man had to be truly desperate to scratch out such a poor living.

So far, he had few leads and several suspects. If displeasure with the work was an indicator, every man here was guilty. Only a few openly talked of unions or against the owner.

He cleaned up as best he could and went to dinner in the longhouse he shared with other unmarried men. He didn't think he could ever scrub away all the coal dust. Every crevice of skin carried a black line as well as around his fingernails. A strong brush and a long soak in a tub of hot water might rid his skin of the grime.

"Gettin' used to the work yet?" James Llewellyn asked as he sat next to him. The Welshman was in Henessy's crew same as Finn and had proven to be a helpful friend who offered advice without belittling Finn.

He dug into his food and shrugged. "But still not liking it overmuch."

The other man laughed. "Who does, lad? We're doomed to be the pawns of the men who own us."

He sent a puzzled glance at his new friend. "No one owns me. Sure and I'm a free man."

The other man gestured to his food. "And that's why you pay twice what this meal's worth for the privilege of eating slop."

Finn laid his fork on his plate. "The charge is more than the food's worth, that's true, but the quality 'tis not that bad." Nothing like he ate while at Dallas and Cenora's, that was certain. But hadn't he had far worse and much less growing up?

The Welshman's mouth twisted in apparent disgust. "Wait until you've had to buy things at the company store. Prices are almost double. The scrip we're paid won't buy much."

Finn picked up his coffee cup. "And you've said no one in the next town will take the scrip."

From his other side, a brown-haired boy no more than seventeen or eighteen said, "Right you are. We're same as prisoners here. Unless you starve yourself, you'll owe more than you can earn. But a job is what I needed and a job is what I found."

"Can nothing be done? Have you complained to the owner?"

Everyone within hearing distance laughed.

The boy rolled his eyes. "Old Farland is the one sets the store's prices and our salaries. He cares naught for us, only for the coal we dig from the ground."

Finn nodded. "I remember hearing miners talk in West Virginia about the same problems."

James narrowed his eyes. "Thought you were from Ireland."

Finn hadn't intended to give away much of himself. "Can you not hear the old country in me voice? But I came several years ago and wandered a bit on the way to where I am. 'Tis a wondrous country."

The boy's eyes lit with interest. "Yeah? What did you do to earn your way?"

"Worked with horses mostly. You know, mucked out stalls and such. I've smelled enough shiite for me lifetime."

James appeared surprised. "You'll likely be doing the same with the mine's animals if they know you've the knack. They have to be cared for."

He ached to free the horses and mules kept underground. "Do they never come out o' the mine?"

His friend said, "Naw. By now they'd be afraid of the light. Probably would blind them."

Finn turned to the brown-haired boy who'd spoken earlier. "Finn O'Neill here. Don't know your name."

"Mick Gallagher from County Cork. I came to start a new life after me family died of typhus. I'm the only one left."

"Sorry, Mick. Tough being on your own, isn't it?" Finn wasn't really on his own, but he'd always felt that way. He was the odd man out in his family, the one who was different, the one who didn't really belong.

Not that his family had ever treated him that way, but he knew in his heart. Instead of the garrulous and good-natured Brendan Sean O'Neill, his father had been a lecherous nobleman who'd forced himself on his mother when she was but a servant girl in his fine manor house. When her resulting pregnancy became obvious, she'd lost her job. If not for Brendan, no telling what would have happened to her—and to Finn.

But Brendan married her, for he'd loved Aoiffe many months. And the kind man insisted Finn was his son in his heart. So, Finn called him Da and tried to fit in.

His brother in law, Dallas, treated him as an equal. From Dallas he'd learned not only to gentle horses with kindness, but also to read and write. What a gift. He rejoiced each time he saw words that no longer looked like so many squiggles to him. Though he still read slowly, he carried a book with him so he could practice whenever he had free time.

After his meal, he stood and joined the other workers. For a couple of hours, they divided into groups. Some played cards, some shot dice. Others went outside to smoke or head for the saloon for a brew. Finn was with the group who sat and talked. How else could he find the information he required?

Joking or cursing their fate, about ten o'clock most made their way to their bunks. Exhaustion lined every face. Finn laid his head on a pillow streaked with coal dust in spite of him trying to clean up each night.

Ladies came in each week to change the sheets and wash the clothes longhouse residents bundled for them. He didn't envy the women's chore. The wash water must turn black immediately. Their job was as bad as his but the laundresses performed theirs on solid ground.

In his quest, he'd focused on two men who might be causing the so-called accidents to hinder the mine. One was Darius Hartford, a man who often mentioned how much a union would help their lives. The other was Council Clayton, one of those suggested by Farland. Finn had learned Clayton had barely escaped being in a cave-in too many times.

Clayton had the knowledge needed to cause the so-called accidents that slowed their progress and had resulted in the death of several men this year. So far, Clayton's own son hadn't joined work in the mines. That fact aroused suspicion among his coworkers that Clayton planned more treachery.

Finn had no proof those or the other two suggested by Farland were up to no good. The chugging of a locomotive ferrying coal from the mine broke into his musing. Worrying about his job and whether or not he'd succeed and get his ranch, he waited for sleep to come. After a hard day's work, the wait was short.

Daylight had yet to arrive when a pounding on the door roused Finn and his coworkers from their beds. They donned their dirty clothes, for there was no point changing into clean ones. He'd learned coal dust soon coated the freshest cloth, so why bother?

That morning, a small, dark-haired man argued with their foreman, Ben Adams. "I tell you, I no want to be in Señor Clayton's crew no more."

"Look, Huerta, you can't switch crews at the drop of a hat."

Finn seized his opportunity. "Mr. Adams, I'll trade with him if doing so saves you trouble."

Adams nodded at Finn. "Thanks. Consider it done." He turned and, after a glare at Juan Huerta, he stomped off.

Finn nodded at the Mexican. "I've been on Henessy's crew over there."

Wondering if he'd made a mistake, he followed his new supervisor into the mine and a different tunnel than where he'd worked before.

Clayton called over his shoulder, "Thanks for diffusing that situation. Sorry to learn Juan believes I'm a jinx. Miners are a superstitious lot."

Finn chuckled. "Me sister's that superstitious, but not meself." He hoped he was the one who was right in the matter. Otherwise, he could be dead by sunset.

Five others picked up their tools and joined them. One, a brooding man whose scowl appeared permanent and who lived in his longhouse, nodded at him as if to acknowledge him. The other three crewmembers eyed him curiously but said nothing. He thought one other of the crew might be in what he thought of as a bunkhouse.

Inside the tunnel opening, water flowed toward the mouth as they walked upward through the mud then along an already worked tunnel. They reached the platform that lowered them into the newer, lower level. He'd never thought himself skittish, but he hated being closed into this place. The swaying as they descended added to his discomfort.

Standing with his new crewmates, Finn had to fight not to flee the rickety cage that jerked and rattled. Two of his coworkers cranked the wheel that lowered them downward into pitch darkness. Anyone shifting his weight increased the swinging and sense of danger. How far would they fall if the wheel slipped or the cable snapped?

Pinpricks of light shone from other crews' lanterns and hats.

Clayton carried the lone Davy lantern that illuminated a spare circle where they stood in the tunnel. After they lit the candles on their hats, their leader sloshed through the ever present water on the floor.

All day Finn stuck close to Council Clayton, but he saw the man do nothing out of the ordinary. Instead, he seemed to work harder than the others. The crew leader had the knack of breaking out the most coal from the seam that varied from three feet to wider than the tunnel. Finn tried to emulate the older man's movements.

When they broke for a rest about noon, Finn sat beside the older man. "Trying to keep up with you is wearing me down, man, and you're almost twice me age. How do you do it?"

Clayton took bread and cheese from his pail. "I've done this since I was waist high. I'd have to be a dunce not to learn by now."

Finn had only bread in his pail, but he tore off a chunk. "Mayhap you could teach me."

"You're catching on just fine. This crew has the best record for the amount of ore. If we keep this up, we'll get a bonus at the end of the month."

"Then I'm glad I changed with Juan. I could use the extra." He swallowed water from his canteen.

Clayton chuckled. "O'Neill, the bonus isn't generous so don't get your hopes too high."

"Still, I might buy me a new set o' clothes to ruin down here."

The other man chuckled and unfolded his lanky body. "All right, men, back to work."

As they left the mine that evening, Finn stayed in step with Clayton. He still hadn't learned anything that would link this man to the mine's troubles. They walked toward the jumble of houses that made up the small town of Lignite. Everything in sight belonged to Farland Coal Mine, and that included the lives of the men.

The crew leader turned to him. "You're welcome to come to dinner with me. Probably nothing but stew, but my wife's a good cook."

Surprised, Finn decided he'd been handed another gift in his quest. "I'd appreciate the chance to dine with a family."

After they pounded dust off their clothes and washed up, Finn followed his host into a company house. Although modest in size, the clapboard structure was one of the larger Lignite homes. He imagined it had three bedrooms instead of the one or two most included.

Inside, a smiling woman greeted them. Gray streaked her auburn hair, but the few lines on her otherwise smooth face proved she smiled a lot. She came to her husband's chin when he leaned down to kiss her.

"Grace love, this is Finn O'Neill. He's now one of my crew and a hard worker."

Finn greeted his hostess and turned at the sound of others entering. A teen-aged boy bounded into the room and sat at the table. Two women glided in. Resembling each other in face and demeanor, one was blonde and one a redhead.

Although both were beautiful, the one with dark red hair captured his attention. She was slim except in the right places. Her greenish-blue eyes met his and held him captive. A light sprinkling of tiny freckles danced across her nose and cheeks.

Beside him, Council Clayton said, "These are my children. Lance, Stella, and Nettie." He repeated what he'd told his wife.

The three murmured greetings in the soft accent of Northern England. Finn didn't know whether he should try to seat the sisters, so he stood behind the spare chair and waited.

Mrs. Clayton smiled at him. "Take your seat, Mr. O'Neill. I'll have dinner on the table in a jiffy."

The redhead named Stella helped her mother carry food while her sister Nettie carried bowls and cutlery.

His hostess proudly took her seat. "You've come on a good day. We have fresh butter for our bread."

Although he'd grown used to the plentiful bounty of his brother in law's ranch, he remembered the lean days before his sister wed Dallas.

"I'm that grateful you'll have me, Mrs. Clayton. If your dinner smells even half as good as the aroma teasing me nose, I'll be in heaven."

Stella sent him a glance that appeared filled with skepticism.

Mrs. Clayton laughed. "Sounds as if you've the taste of Irish blarney on your tongue."

Council chuckled and patted his wife's hand. "My Grace's food is every bit as good as it smells."

She ladled thick stew into their bowls. Stella sliced a round loaf of bread and passed the tray around. Next came the butter. Finn took a spare amount for he realized the spread was a precious commodity.

He couldn't help glancing at the gorgeous Stella. What was wrong with him? He'd vowed he'd never let himself be attracted to a woman with hair like his sister Cenora's. Didn't he know well enough the fiery temper that accompanied that color? Hadn't he experienced how the rough edge of his sister's tongue cut into a man?

What was he to do? Da always told him to 'never say never' about anything. Now he realized how true the saying. Something about the lovely redhead called to his soul.

Stella had mesmerized him with her sparkling blue-green eyes and skin as smooth and delicate as the finest cream. Her voice carried a musical lilt that had him aching to hear her speak more. She might as well have trussed him up like a fat goose for he was same as cooked.

Nettie was just as pretty, maybe prettier, but he couldn't keep his eyes from straying back to her sister. He forced himself to look anywhere else. He'd best gather his wits and get on to the business of learning what he needed.

Although he knew the answer, he addressed a question to Lance, "And do you work in the mines as well?"

Lance looked at his food. "Not yet."

Stella scowled. "And he never will if I have my way."

Council stared at her. "Remember we have a guest, daughter."

"Sorry, Papa." But she didn't appear sorry. Instead, her pretty face set in determination.

Finn figured this was an old argument he'd best not join. "Mrs. Clayton, the stew is even better than the glorious aroma promised. Don't know when I've tasted better bread either."

His hostess beamed. "Why, thank you. Only simple fare, but you're welcome here."

Nettie smiled mischievously at him. "Stella baked the bread."

Stella gaped at her sister. "Because it was my turn. You bake just as well."

"No, she don't." Lance shook his head and shoved more food into his mouth.

Didn't he remember that lads that age were always hungry? Grasping at another subject, Finn asked, "How long have you lived here?"

Council set down his spoon. "If you mean America or Lignite, the answer's the same. I was hired by Mr. Farland from our home near Newcastle, England a year ago. He needed experienced miners to work here and I fit the bill."

Mrs. Clayton smiled proudly at her husband. "We'd always talked of coming to America, you see, so the offer seemed a godsend because Mr. Farland paid our fare. Mr. Farland even offered my husband a job as night foreman. Thankfully, he chose to work days."

Stella opened her mouth as if to speak, but apparently changed her mind. He understood that she didn't like mining. Darned if he didn't agree with her.

His hostess continued. "Stella and Nettie teach school here. Mr. Farland lets them use a building up the hill. Stella takes the older students and Nettie the youngest."

Finn raised his eyebrows. Didn't he admire anyone able to teach others? "Good to know there's a school. Reading and writing are valuable tools for life."

Stella sent him a puzzled glance. "Yes, and most of their parents can't teach them because they don't know how themselves. Many don't speak English."

"'Tis a fine job you're doing then. But I thought many o' the boys went to work early in the mine. How old are the students you teach?"

"Nettie takes those aged five to seven and has to teach most of them to speak English. I have those eight and older. Mainly the older students are girls because many families don't value education and let the boys stop school at age ten."

"If I'd had a chance, I'd have gone to school as long as I could."

She sent him an inquiring stare. "Oh, and just how long did you go?"

He set down his mug. "Miss Clayton, when I was a boy in Ireland, the Irish weren't allowed to attend school. What I know, me father and brother in law taught me. I practice me reading whenever I can." He smiled to soften his words.

She blushed. "I'm sorry. I didn't know, and find that horrid. No one should be denied an education."

"I agree, but no one consulted me." She might be English, but 'twas not her who forbid him a chance to learn. Anyway, he wouldn't have had many years in school before his family was tossed off their land. Best not to dwell on his past.

His host clapped him on the shoulder. "Come sit in the parlor a spell."

The men rose while the women cleaned the kitchen. Finn took a ladder-back chair near the unlit stove. The sparse furnishings had only one chair with arms, a bench, and the chair in which he sat.

He asked, "Did I take your wife's chair?"

Clayton waved away his question. "No matter. Lance, bring a chair from the kitchen."

The boy rose quickly to do his father's bidding.

Finn stared at figures on a shelf. "Did you make those?"

Figures depicting children and animals formed a line. The figures had features and details the attested to the creator's skill. His favorite was a girl with flowing hair and twirling dress. Finn could picture Stella as a child in that pose.

His host gestured to them. "Carving the coal is a way to pass the time of a Sunday afternoon. Several of the men do the same."

"You've talent. Do you sell them?"

Clayton appeared surprised at the question. "Never considered anyone would want one."

"I'd like the one o' the little girl and o' the dog."

A broad smile split Clayton's face. "The girl is my wife's favorite. She thinks the girl looks like one of ours. Since we aren't supposed to have pets here, I gave Lance the dog."

Lance laughed. "I call him Spot."

Finn considered his words. "I understand there was an accident in the tunnel recently. The men say you saved lives that day."

Council took his pipe from the shelf, sat in the high-backed chair, and filled it. "Some say so. Others say I jinxed them by being nearby." He lit the tobacco.

"You work twice as hard as most. Perhaps they speak from jealousy."

Resting his head against the back of his chair, his host puffed and exhaled a cloud of smoke. "I've been nearby when three accidents happened but haven't been caught in the debris. Apparently that's enough to cause the talk."

"Rumor can slaughter a man's reputation. Have you tried to combat the claims?"

The other man met his gaze. "How? Once the story starts, it has a life of its own."

"You have a point. 'Tis a problem and that's the truth o' the matter."

The women came in and settled their skirts around them. With the limberness of youth, Lance sat cross legged on the floor.

Mrs. Clayton gestured to the mandolin in the corner. "Papa, why don't you play us a tune?"

"Ah, I've not the strength tonight, love."

Finn gazed at the instrument. "If you've no objection, I'll play. 'Tis yearning I've been to have a chance. I miss having me own instrument."

With a nod from Council, he took the mandolin and strummed the keys to tune them. Then he launched into a cheerful tune and sang along. The family appeared pleased at his efforts. On the next tune, the sisters joined in.

After four songs, he stood and set the instrument aside. "Thank you. 'Tis the finest evening I've had in many. Good food, good company, and good music. What more can any man ask?"

Pushing up from the chair, Council stretched, bones popping in the process. He extended his hand. "You must come again sometime."

"'Twill be me pleasure. I'll see you tomorrow before the sun has a chance to show its face."

What an evening. He'd had a fine dinner with two beautiful women present, though 'twas the redhead Stella that set his blood pumping. He laughed at himself for his foolish thoughts. Cocking his hat on his head, he shoved his hands in his pockets and whistled a tune on his way to the longhouse.

After his time on the ranch, he thought of the place as a bunkhouse. The building housed twenty bunks for as many men with a dining hall at one end. Another like it stood nearby for the single men who worked at night. As much as he hated his job, he thought the night crew would be worse.

The hairs on the back of his neck bristled.

Someone followed him. When he slowed, so did the person behind him. Sure and he was glad Dallas had insisted he conceal a knife in one boot and an ankle gun in the other. But if someone knocked him in the head, what chance would he have to use either?

With relief, he reached the longhouse and paused near the door to peer around. He saw nothing untoward, so he slipped quietly inside. From the loud snores and coughing, he figured most were already asleep except for a few who played cards at one end of the long room.

He slid off his clothes and sprawled out on his bunk. Stacking his hands beneath his head, he stared at the inky shadows. A few minutes later James and Mick stumbled in. Mick was in his cups and leaned on James, who appeared sober.

When he'd dumped Mick on a bed, James undressed. As he plopped on his bed next to Finn's, he asked, "Where were you all day?"

Finn explained about the change in crew. "Had a nice evening at his house, too."

"You're brave to risk working with Clayton. Most think the man's a jinx."

"So I've heard, but I don't believe in such. A man makes his own luck when he can."

James turned his head to meet Finn's gaze. "Exactly. Which is why others wonder if he's a bit too lucky because he's helping the 'accidents' happen."

"You think he's causing them? Why would he do that?" He asked in spite of the same thoughts in his mind.

"He could be on the side of the unions. Or he could be working for a rival mine company."

"I'll have to see evidence before I believe either claim." After an evening in the man's home, he felt honor bound to defend him.

"By the way, Finn. I've my eye on Stella Clayton, so don't get ideas in that direction."

"Meanin' no offense, James, but 'tis her place to warn me off. I'll stay away when she tells me."

Chapter Three

On Sunday, his day off, Finn walked the two miles to the next town, which was Spencer. The weather was fine with a cloudless blue sky and the hint of fall in the air. After a week underground, he took pleasure in the breeze that cooled the sun's rays and the soft earth that cushioned his feet. This was his first time to stroll around Spencer.

He found a butcher right away and saved the spot for later, grateful that several places were open today. Last night he'd penned letters and now he dropped them at the tiny post office area of the general store and bought stamps. One was his report to Farland, one a letter to Grandpa McClintock, and the other he'd written to his sister.

She'd share the news with their parents and his brother Mac and Mac's wife Vourneen. 'Twas a grand feeling to be able to write his thoughts to Cenora and know she could read them all those miles away. Her marryin' Dallas had opened up a world of opportunities for the O'Neil family. Learning to read was only one of many.

Trying to remember the prices he'd seen in the Lignite company store, he compared them to those here in Spencer. The outrageous difference in charges made him angry. Farland should be helping his employees instead of skinning them of their meager pay. Finn was grateful he had with him a portion of his earnings paid by Dallas.

Whimsy overtook him and he couldn't resist a length of green ribbon that matched the color of Stella's blue-green eyes and one of blue for her sister Nettie. To keep things even, he purchased a length of lavender for Mrs. Clayton. He found a package of pipe tobacco he thought the senior Clayton would enjoy. What would he get Lance?

A book called *Tom Sawyer* caught his eye. For himself, he bought a sarsaparilla, a length of red licorice. As he paid for his purchases, something caught his eye behind the owner.

"Is that concertina for sale?"

The owner, Mr. George, turned and took the dusty instrument off the shelf. "Took this thing in exchange for food six months ago. If you're interested, I'll make you a good price."

"Aye, unless the bellows have holes or the keys don't work, I'm interested." He unfastened the strap binding the concertina closed and played a tune.

He closed the instrument and fastened the leather that held the bellows closed. "Appears to work fine even though 'tis dusty and the bellows are old. What's your price?"

When he and Mr. George struck a deal, Finn laughed at the dusty concertina, thinking of the music still left in the old instrument.

Feeling a fool for his purchases, he stopped by the butcher and bought a smoke-cured ham. He was being foolish, but he appreciated the kindness the Claytons had shown him. 'Twas more than anyone else in Lignite had done.

Or, perhaps he was paying off his conscience in case he found Council Clayton guilty of accusations he'd heard.

Lugging his purchases back to Lignite, he pondered his findings. One, many were suspicious of Clayton. That could be partly because of him being English. Sure and the Irish and Welsh were never overly fond of the English.

Three cave-ins were a puzzle. Clayton had been inside but had been spared while other crews were injured or killed. But he hadn't actually been in the fall. Was that coincidence or by devious design? Either way seemed just as risky.

Two, someone had followed Finn after he'd left the Clayton home. The person couldn't have been Clayton or one of his family members. Three, there was mischief afoot yet he hadn't made enough headway to satisfy himself or Farland. No doubt there'd be a terse letter waiting for him on his next trip to Spencer.

Back in Lignite, he stopped by Council Clayton's home. Lance opened the door.

He handed over the ham, book, tobacco, and ribbons. "I wanted to thank your family for the fine evening I had the other night."

"For us?" Obviously perplexed, Lance gathered the gifts to his body.

"Aye, I went to Spencer with a few coins in me pockets and felt the need to spend them. I hope you enjoy the result. The book's for you. Tell your kind mother the lavender ribbon is for her and the other bits are for your sisters."

He walked toward the longhouse, whistling a fine ditty. Didn't he feel like dancing a jig on the way? To prove it, he broke into a few steps.

He could picture the green ribbon against the red of Stella's hair.

Sure and her eyes were more green than blue. But what if she chose the blue ribbon? No matter, 'twould look as lovely.

The next morning, he showed up at the usual time of six.

Clayton pulled him aside, a frown marring his brow. "What were you thinking to be wasting your hard earned scrip on others?"

"Sure and I meant no harm. I've missed eating at a table with family. You were kind to me and I saw a few things in the Spencer store that I bought to repay your kindness."

Clayton appeared surprised. "Spencer? You had cash then?"

"Aye, I'd a bit put by before I came here. Spending it gave me pleasure and I hope you received the small gifts the same way."

His supervisor nodded. "Your generosity pleased us all. Maybe you'll come to dinner on Sunday and we'll have the ham."

A chance to see Stella again, just as he'd hoped. Plus mayhap he could find out more about his crew boss. "Sure and 'twould be a treat."

"After church about one then. Now we'd best get busy."

The other five men on the crew sent pointed looks his way, so Finn worked even harder to prove he was no slacker or boot licker. Aleski Karpinski was the crew member whose black looks concerned Finn. By the end of the day, he could barely stagger to his longhouse but darned if he hadn't helped set a record for the day. The others should be happy to have him for he'd done his part to insure them their bonus.

***

Stella held the green ribbon in her hands. "What sort of man spends his money on people he's just met? Why isn't he saving for the future?"

Her sister tied the blue ribbon around her hair. "Can't you take pleasure in the gift instead of questioning the giver?"

"Harrumph. I suppose you're sweet on him?"

Nettie's eyes sparkled when she glanced at Stella. "You're the one he couldn't take his eyes from that night. I wonder what James Llewellyn would think of that?"

As if she cared. She supposed Mr. Llewellyn was nice enough, but she was standing firm in her beliefs. "What Mr. Llewellyn thinks is not important to me. I'm not marrying a miner, and that's final. I'd rather be an old maid."

Nettie examined her image in the mirror and adjusted the bow on her ribbon. "Too bad. Considering our current lack of non-miner suitors, that may be your only choice. Unless you're interested in the reverend, and he's over sixty if he's a day." She giggled.

Standing behind her sister, Stella smoothed her own dark red hair. "I'm serious, Nettie. I simply have to find a better life than this."

The other woman twirled away. "You could be starving on a dirt farm somewhere with a dull farmer and six kids."

Stella slipped on her shoes and pretended the soles weren't so worn. She dreaded winter when she'd feel every cold stone in spite of the cardboard she'd slid inside. "What a picture that is. But a farmer at least has a large garden and animals with plenty to eat."

Nettie laughed from the doorway. "So you'll be fat but barefoot and work from sunup to sundown and never finish with your chores."

She couldn't help grinning at her sister. "You are terrible, you know. Hurry so we won't be late for school." They left the house and linked arms.

All day, Stella couldn't get the picture of the handsome Irishman from her mind. His dark hair and flashing eyes haunted her. How wonderful to learn he loved music as much as she did. Every day she missed the piano they'd had to leave behind in England.

To think he hadn't learned to read in school. She'd never thought about the English laws affecting the Irish. Had she ever known about the one concerning schooling? Surely not or she'd have remembered something that important. Knowing now embarrassed her for her former country.

Mr. O'Neill was taller than Papa but not by much. She guessed he'd be about five feet and eleven inches, four inches taller than she was. About the right difference to kiss. Her cheeks heated at the turn of her thoughts. Good heavens, she was worse about daydreaming than the girls she taught.

Neither she nor Nettie received any pay for teaching. She hoped they were at least making a difference in lives. Barring that, perhaps she was gathering experience that would get her a genuine paying job soon.

On Sunday, Stella was a bundle of nerves. Although he was coming to eat with her family, she was as giddy as if Finn O'Neill were coming to see her. Her footsteps were light as she busied herself helping her mother make early preparations for lunch.

She washed her hands and dried them. "Well, that's taken care of. Are you ready for church?"

"Stella, what are you thinking?"

She looked up to find her mother staring at her. "What?"

Mama pointed at her. "Are you going to church in your

nightclothes?"

Her cheeks heated as she rushed to the bedroom she shared with her sister. She threw off her wrapper and grabbed Nettie's arm. "Hurry. Help me get dressed."

She sped through her toilette and Nettie laced her into her corset. No time to create a fancy hairdo. She swirled her tresses into a bun. No, she wanted to wear the ribbon, so she combed out her long hair and let it hang loose down her back. With her shawl temporarily covering her head, she walked with her family to the Protestant church beside the Catholic chapel. Farland Mine Company provided both buildings.

All the way to church she argued with herself. She would never be interested in a miner. Not even a handsome one with dark flashing eyes and a pleasing lilt in his speech. Quite the contrary to his angelic singing voice, she suspected Finn O'Neill was full of the devil.

Chapter Four

Finn rose early and walked to Spencer to collect his mail and send another report to Farland. The more he learned of the mine owner's practices, the less he liked the man—and he hadn't liked him in the first place. Farland had trouble coming to him and there was nothing Finn could do to prevent all of the problems the owner had created. His only job was to find the one deliberately endangering lives and causing delays.

When Mr. George handed Finn his mail, he found a rude note from Farland telling him to speed up his investigation. Blast the man. If he wanted faster, he could search for himself. Only the lure of Lippincott's ranch kept Finn in the hellhole called Farland Coal Mine.

Finn shopped through the mercantile without finding what he sought until he stood at the counter. "I'll take that box o' candy." 'Twould do to take the entire Clayton family.

Back in Lignite, he washed his hands and gathered his concertina before making his way to the Claytons' home, happy to avoid James and his warning to stay away from Stella.

Church was still meeting when he reached the Claytons' home, so he set on the porch steps and enjoyed the morning. The smell of flowers growing on either side of the porch filled the air. Their bright heads waved cheerfully on green stalks. He wondered at their names.

Soon, the family members walked toward him. He stood and waited to be invited inside. Once there, he presented his hostess with the candy.

"Why, thank you, Mr. O'Neill. I-I don't think we've had store-bought chocolates since we've been in America. But the girls made a cobbler for dessert."

"Oh, 'tis not for our meal, ma'am. 'Tis for the family's pleasure some other time."

Stella met his gaze. "And what did you buy for yourself?"

He glanced at the fingers he'd recently washed after his snack. "Pickled eggs, a sticky bun, and a sarsaparilla."

She raised an eyebrow. "Not beer or whiskey?"

What a snappish woman, but he enjoyed her challenge. "Not

every Irishman drinks to excess any more than every school teacher is frumpy and unmarriageable."

Stella gasped but her family laughed.

Her sister said, "Guess you'll learn not to be so shrewish."

Stella blushed. "I suppose that was rude, but I must insist I hadn't intended my question as such."

Her father shook his head. "Which made it even ruder, daughter. When will you learn to think before you speak?"

Mrs. Clayton set the candy on a side table. "Girls, hurry and let's get the meal dished up so we can eat. I don't know about the others, but I'm famished."

After a short blessing, they passed around bowls and the meat platter. Finn took servings of potatoes, ham, corn, and beans.

Mrs. Clayton said, "When we didn't see you in church, we thought perhaps you'd gone to the Catholic chapel."

Finn almost said he attended the Presbyterian Church at home and only caught himself in the nick of time. "I had an errand in Spencer this morning. 'Tis where I get me mail and I'd hoped for a letter from me sister."

"Is she still in Ireland?" Stella asked.

He didn't want to lie, so he skirted the question. "Me sister's married and expecting her first. I thought mayhap she'd be letting me know I'm an uncle but I was disappointed. I'll check again next Sunday."

Before the inquisitive woman across the table could ask another probing question, he asked his own. "Do most o' the miners attend church?"

Mrs. Clayton shook her head. "No, only a few single men and about half the families. Most use the day to rest."

"Well, 'twas what the Lord did after workin' six days. Still, mayhap next week I'll save me errands for the afternoon."

Lance asked, "Wasn't that a concertina you set down in the parlor?"

"Aye. The Spencer store had an old one someone had traded for food. Sad when a man has to trade music for sustenance, but 'twas gatherin' dust on a shelf. The store owner made me a good price."

Clayton laughed. "Didn't want to let anyone interested escape without a sale, eh?"

Finn smiled broadly. "Right you are and I was that happy he was agreeable. Da has one, for all me family are musical. Ma and I play the fiddle and all the menfolk play bodrán drum, concertina, fiddle, and uilleann bagpipes. Me sister sings like an angel and dances."

The other man nodded. "And what does your father do for a job?"

"He's a farmer." Finn laughed. "But his main occupation is talking a blue streak, such as I'm doing now. He's that full of the blarney he can charm the birds from the trees."

Stella raised an eyebrow. "I think you've also a touch of the blarney."

Her mother gasped and glared at her. "Stella, I declare you sound as if you've not been taught manners."

Finn held up his hand, ignoring the fact Mrs. Clayton had accused him of the same thing last time he was here. "No offense taken, Mrs. Clayton."

To Stella, he said, "You've not heard Da speak or you'd make no comparison. He has an Irish blessing for every occasion and can expound for hours with little provocation. Sure and the Lord gave Da the gift o' gab like no other man before or since."

After sending a glance toward her mother, Stella met his gaze. "I apologize if I sounded critical. Easy to understand you miss seeing your family. As exasperating as I find mine sometimes, I'd miss them if we weren't together."

"Aye, I do yearn to see them. 'Tis grand to be included here today, for your fine companionship has softened my longing."

His hostess beamed. "What a lovely thing to say, Mr. O'Neill. We're pleased to have you share in your generous gift of this ham. How about some apple cobbler for dessert?"

"Wouldn't that be lovely?" Finn's mouth watered at the thought. He'd curbed his appetite and not eaten much ham. He understood how precious meat was to this family.

After they'd all had apple cobbler, Council looked at his mandolin. "Shall we see if we can make music?"

"Aye, I'd hoped you'd be in the mood today." He followed the other man to the parlor.

The women hastily put away the remaining food and washed the dishes. Finn picked up his concertina and took a seat on the bench. His host sat by the stove and strummed on his mandolin.

Council nodded to him. "You start off and I'll try to follow."

Tapping his foot, Finn played "Rocky Road to Dublin." When it appeared by his host's puzzled expression that he didn't know that song,

Finn switched to "Oh! Susanna" and Council joined in.

When she came into the parlor, Stella sat beside him on the bench. He took that as a good sign and his heart swelled. The women joined in singing. The two men had played four songs when there was a loud knock.

Lance hopped up to answer the door. James Llewellyn entered. Abruptly, Finn ceased playing.

James stood with a bouquet of wildflowers in one hand. He looked accusingly at Stella then glared at Finn. "Looks as if you've a party in progress. Sorry to interrupt." His facial expression left no doubt he was glad he'd intruded.

Council stood and offered James his hand, which James shook. "Not a party, but a little impromptu music to brighten the day. Lance, bring another chair from the kitchen."

James handed the flowers to Stella. "Thanks but I can get my own chair." James fairly stomped to retrieve a seat that he placed as near Stella's place on the bench as he could. Then he sat, glowering at Finn.

Stella hopped up. "I'll just put the flowers in water. Thank you, Mr. Llewellyn."

Finn bore no guilt for visiting the Claytons, but James's appearance cast a pall over his pleasant afternoon. From the bitter looks the other man sent his way, he was as unhappy having Finn there as Finn was to see him.

Stella returned with a clear canning jar filled with water and the flowers. She sat them on a shelf by the stove and turned. "There, I believe everyone can see them now. Aren't they pretty?"

James' expression softened. "I know how you like flowers, but not many are blooming this late. Mrs. Potts let me cut some of her roses."

Tension still sparked around the room. Stella appeared about to jump out of her skin. Nettie's eyes sparkled with what looked like mischievous mirth at her sister's discomfort. No matter how much a body loved a sister, didn't he know how vexing one could be?

To diffuse the awkwardness, Finn nodded to Council and broke into "Camptown Races" and Council joined him. Next, Finn sang as he played "Last Rose of Summer". He smiled at Stella and suspected he angered James more for the reference. Stella blushed prettily, which must have irked James even more.

After half an hour, he paused. "Sure and it's been a lovely afternoon, but I'd best be getting on before I wear out me welcome.

Mayhap everyone will join in a last song and sing the parts to 'Whispering Hope.' 'Tis Ma's favorite and 'tis suitable for a Sunday."

Each of the Claytons chimed in on the two-part harmony. Apparently James didn't know the words but he added his efforts, off key and always slightly behind. Finn and Council's tenor voices harmonized on the refrain and Lance joined them. The women's sang clear and sweet.

Afterward, Finn collapsed his concertina and fastened the strap that held it closed.

Stella clasped her hands against her chest. "That was lovely. What a pleasant afternoon we've shared."

Finn stood and nodded toward Mrs. Clayton. "Thank you for having me in your home today." He turned to Council. "I'll see you tomorrow."

"And I'll see you later, James." With a glance at James, who seemed determined to remain, Finn left the Claytons and walked back to the bunkhouse.

He feared he'd made an enemy of James. Be that as it may, he had no intention of staying away from the Clayton home. Even if he hadn't wanted to learn more about the father, he was firmly smitten by the lovely Stella.

Inside the bunkhouse, several miners played poker. They'd turned a barrel on end for a table and had found three stools and two chairs. Finn stood behind Mick Gallagher, aware Aleski Karpinski won most hands. Although Finn paid close attention, he detected nothing to indicate Karpinski cheated. Mayhap the man was that skillful. But was he skillful at cards or at cheating?

Mick Gallagher lost most of his pay. He threw down his cards and leaped to his feet. "No man is that lucky. I think you're cheating, Karpinski."

The Pole stood, dwarfing Mick. "I've no need to cheat. Admit you're a bad player, lad, and I'll let your insult slide this time."

Mick turned red and opened his mouth, but Finn grabbed his arm. "Sure and Mick meant no harm, Aleski. Come with me, Mick, for I've a need to ask you something."

Finn fairly dragged Mick to the end of the bunkhouse. "What are you thinking, you crazy Irishman, to challenge a man twice your size?"

Mick jerked free. "He cheated me and I want my scrip back."

Finn stepped forward and peered into Mick's face. "Lad, didn't I watch the game? He didn't cheat. Mayhap he's that good at cards."

"Ha, maybe he's that good at cheating."

Finn sat on his bunk. "If you can't afford to lose, don't play. That's the way o' life, Mick."

The younger man gaped at him, his face red again. "You're taking his side? I thought you were me friend."

He pointed at Mick. "I'm a better friend than you know. Aleski could smash you into the floor with one fist. And his friends are near as strong. Don't you know not to start a fight when you've no chance of winning?"

Mick stood with feet braced and arms crossed. "You think I'm afraid? I'm not."

"Sure and you should be. There's a time to fight and a time to back away. In the future, mind you know the difference."

Mick turned and stormed out of the bunkhouse. The lad appeared near tears, angry and humiliated. Mayhap a walk would cool him down enough to see reason.

Mick reminded Finn of his hot tempered brother, Mac. Hadn't he made a habit of keeping Mac out of scrapes most of their lives? He'd no wish to exchange one troublemaker for another, but he couldn't stand by and let Mick talk himself into a beating.

Finn wandered back to watch the card game. He never played except to win and he knew he wasn't as good as Aleski. What he didn't know was whether Aleski was that good at playing or cheating.

The large man met his gaze. "Want to join us, O'Neill?"

"I know not to pit meself against a player good as you. I intend to keep me scrip until the store manager cheats me out of it."

Aleski laughed. "Smart man. But I heard you have real money. I'd like some of that for a change."

Alarm shot through Finn. Where had that rumor started? He feigned indifference and laughed. "Then you're working at the wrong place, man. 'Tis in short supply here."

Aleski dealt another round of cards to the men gathered around the upturned barrel. "Where'd you come by yours?"

"Training horses. Hard work but I saved a little o' me money."

Play resumed and Finn continued to watch. He noted the habits of each man. Pakulski rubbed his chin when he had a good hand. Gundersen pulled at his ear when he had a winning hand. Bosko drummed his fingers when he had a good hand.

Aleski gave nothing away. Mayhap Aleski was a cool enough head to be up to mischief as Farland accused.

Finn was tired of mining for coal. He hated being trapped underground all day. He went to work before sunup and emerged after dusk. Only on Sunday could he enjoy the light of day.

Without the lure of Lippincott's ranch, he would have quit the first day. Thinking of the prize green pastures, large house, and strong barns kept him searching for troublemakers. He wondered if Grandpa would honor the loan if no culprit was discovered?

Grandpa had said he would see Lippincott that day, but what did that mean? Did Grandpa buy the ranch for himself or for Finn? The prime property would make a grand investment for Grandpa. Worry ate at his gut and his insides coiled tighter than a spring.

He hated that his suspicions here included Council Clayton. The man had need of extra money to care for his family, that was certain. Would he jeopardize the mine for someone else?

He supposed he'd best go looking for Mick and make sure the young man wasn't in trouble. As angry as Mick had been, he wouldn't be watching where he stepped. The boyo could stumble and roll down a hill. Finn turned and headed for the door.

Finn strode from the long frame building and peered around. He heard a yell and headed in the direction he thought the call had originated. The cry came again and Finn broke into a run.

He stopped at a mine tunnel vent hole.

Peering inside, he could see nothing. "Mick? Are you down there?"

"O'Neill, is that you? Help me."

He knelt, hoping to see something. "Are you hurt?"

"Fall broke my leg."

"I'll get rope and help and I'll hurry back." Finn rose to his feet.

He raced to the longhouse and called to the card players. "Mick fell down a vent hole. Where can I find rope? And I need a few o' you to help."

The card players threw down their cards and one gathered money.

Karpinski was first up to help. "Is he conscious?"

"Yeah, but he thinks his leg is broken. Kid's sounds scared half to death."

"We can get rope from the supply shed. Go talk to calm him and we'll be along soon enough."

Finn hurried back to the opening. How could Mick have

stumbled in?

"Mick, some o' the men are getting rope and tools to get you out. Stay calm, lad."

"Hurry, I'm hurtin' bad, man."

"They're coming. Don't try to move."

The sound of feet pounding caused Finn to turn. "They're here, Mick. We'll have you out in no time."

Aleski lit a lantern and tied a rope around the handle. "I'll lower the light so we can see what we're up against."

When he'd dropped the lamp down the hole, Aleski raised his head and exchanged a look with Finn. "We have a difficult job ahead of us."

Finn stared at the pinpoint of light on the narrow ledge twenty feet below. A few inches to the left and Mick would have fallen at least into inky blackness. Finn took up another length of rope and made a loop.

Lying on his stomach, he peered into the hole. "Put the loop I'm lowering around you under your arms and we'll pull you up."

Mick reached for the loop and missed. He nearly fell off the ledge. As the loop swung by, he grabbed the line. Within seconds he had pulled it over his head and shoulders and secured it under his arms.

"I'm ready. Don't drop the rope."

Finn guided the line as three men behind him hauled the young man to the top. Finn grasped his shoulders and pulled him free. He lay on the ground and rolled away from the gaping maw that had almost cost him his life.

Aleski raised the lantern. "Say, Irish, guess you'll learn to look where you're going in the future."

"The hole was covered with dirt on a tarp. When I put my foot down, the tarp gave way and I fell."

Aleski gave a derisive grunt. "You must be mistaken. Why would anyone do such a thing?"

Mick's voice quavered. "I'm telling the truth."

Finn lowered the light again. "The boy's right. I see a piece o' canvas on the ledge."

Aleski and a couple of the men joined Finn in peering into the pit.

The big Pole pushed against his knees then unbent his large frame to stand away from the gaping hole. "That's a devil of a thing to do. And where's the pole and flag meant to keep such from happening?"

One of his friends pointed to the ground. "Here's where the pole stood. See the hole? It's been removed on purpose."

Finn helped Mick to his good foot and held him upright. "Is there an infirmary or hospital in Lignite?"

Aleski supported Mick's other arm over his shoulder. "Doctor comes from Spencer but there's a sick ward west of the longhouse."

Together they half-carried the young Irishman to a place where he could rest and await the doctor. The small building housed four bunks, two of which were occupied. Finn and Aleski lowered Mick to a bed and tried to make him as comfortable as possible.

Aleski said, "Sorry I doubted you, Gallagher. I'll walk to Spencer and rouse the doctor."

When the Pole had gone, Finn pulled a chair near the younger man's bed. "Can you think who would set such a trap for the unwary?"

"Whoever is causing the trouble. I don't know if the problem is from those who want a union or against Farland. Too many things have been happening for coincidence."

He poured a glass of water and brought it to Mick. "This was downright evil and intended to kill. Although you don't feel it now, you're lucky you hit the ledge. 'Twas a long way to the bottom and you'd be dead by now."

"You're right, I don't feel lucky. I lost most of me scrip and now I'm laid up and can't earn more."

"Sure and I'm that sorry. Try to stay calm and rest until the doctor comes. Now I'd best learn if other holes have been covered as traps. I'll check on you tomorrow."

Finn headed to the Clayton home. Wondering if James was still sitting with Stella, he rapped on the door. When Lance answered, he asked to speak to his father.

Council stepped to the doorway. Finn gestured him outside and explained what had happened. "Do you know where other vent holes are located?"

"That I do. They're marked by poles with a flag attached. Follow me." He strode off.

Finn hurried beside him. "The pole and flag had been removed from the hole where Mick through. Likely the same is true o' the others."

They located the three other openings, each of which was covered by canvas on which dirt had been spread to camouflage the deceit. The pole and flag for each had been tossed to the side. Council yanked each covering off. At each place, Council replaced the four-foot high marker with a yellow flag attached.

By the third time, Council's anger appeared to have gone from simmer to rage. "If I discover who did this, I swear I'll wring his neck then throw him down one of these holes."

"I understand how you feel. Poor Mick Gallagher will be off work for a long time."

"He's fortunate to be alive." Council let the way back toward his home.

Finn noted James walking toward the bunkhouse. "Sure and didn't I tell him the same? He doesn't feel lucky right now. He's in a lot of pain. I hope you'll report this to the owner."

Council appeared grim in the oncoming dusk. "Yes, I don't know that he can do anything more than pay the doctor to set the boy's leg. And he'll probably charge Gallagher for that. He's not…um, not the most considerate man. Since this will slow his schedule, he'll be angry."

"He'll not take this out on you, will he? 'Tis not your fault."

"Ah, but he'll want to blame someone. Sometimes that's the messenger."

"Well, I'll see you in the mornin'." Finn stuffed his hands in his pockets and strolled in the direction of the bunkhouse deep in thought.

Who would gain by causin' death and accidents in Lignite? How was he supposed to ferret out the truth? He was almost positive Council and Aleski were innocent. On the other hand, a clever man would appear so, wouldn't he?

Chapter Five

Monday afternoon, Stella trudged beside her sister after a difficult day teaching. Another of her students, fourteen-year-old Peter Swensen, had quit to follow his father and older brother into the mine. In her head, she knew the world required lignite coal for fuel. At the same time, her heart broke at the thought of another boy leaving school for a future of backbreaking labor with little reward and usually a shortened life span.

As they walked, Nettie asked, "Did you know the man who was injured yesterday?"

"No, did you?"

"I heard he lives in the same longhouse as James Llewellyn and Finn O'Neill, but I can't place him. Perhaps if we saw him we'd recognize him."

"Mama's probably been to see the poor man today." Stella admired the compassion their sweet mother displayed for those less fortunate.

Once again, she vowed to do everything in her power to keep Lance from joining their father in the mine. Lance was intelligent and somewhat sensitive. His physique was on the smallish side. She loved him and fought to protect him. He belonged in university studying to be a doctor or lawyer or something else that would benefit mankind.

Nettie glanced at her. "What are you going to do about Mr. Llewellyn? He's quite smitten with you. I thought he'd punch Mr. O'Neill when he saw him in our parlor."

Stella shrugged. "There's nothing to be done. Although I've never been openly rude to the man, I've done nothing to encourage him, nor will I. You know very well my view about miners."

"Yes, but I want a home and a family some day, don't you?"

"Of course, but not with a miner. We're going to take the state teacher's exam so we can get jobs as real teachers with pay. Not much of a salary, I'll admit, but we'll be treated with respect and meet men in an ordinary community."

They were treated with respect by most of the mining community now. Even though there was no value placed on education in this town, people appeared to look up to anyone who could teach reading and writing. She wished more miners sent their children to school. The miners apparently believed there was no point in learning things not needed for work. And every man they knew was a miner.

Nettie sighed dreamily. "I hope we can manage a post for the coming school year. Wouldn't that be wonderful?"

"Heavenly. Too early to submit applications now. In April or May, we can send letters."

"Poor Mama. She'll hate losing both of us at the same time."

"Both leaving the same week is unlikely, but I know she'll miss us and we'll miss her and Papa and Lance. I hope we get a post close enough to visit. Either way, that will mean she and Papa will have more money with two less to feed and clothe and more time for one another."

"For one another?" Nettie lowered her voice. "You don't think they still…, you know, do you? I mean, Lance is sixteen so surely not."

Stella gasped and punched her sister's arm. "Nettie Sue Clayton. You do think of the most astonishing things."

"Don't tell me you've never wondered the same thing."

Stella giggled. "What if I have? Mama is thirty-eight. That's the same age as Mrs. Miller who just had another baby."

Nettie's eyes widened and she grabbed her sister's arm. "You don't think Mama would have another child, do you? That would be awful."

"Oh, I hope she doesn't. I'm only saying people of that age must still…you know, or Mrs. Miller wouldn't have a new little boy."

"To go with the nine she already had. Where do they all eat and sleep?" After a few more steps, Nettie asked, "Do you ever wonder what being with a man would be like?"

"Sometimes. Don't you?"

"Lots of times. But I haven't met anyone who strikes my fancy. Not like you and Mr. O'Neill. You look at one another a little bit like Mama and Papa do."

Stella concealed her surprise. She had sensed a connection with him, but suspected he was merely flirting. Certainly she had no intention of betraying her interest. "Nonsense, you're letting your romantic nature run away imaging things. He's a miner and I'll never consider a miner as a husband."

"No, I watched both of you Sunday. The look on your faces was as if an invisible cord stretched between you. I hope that happens to me someday."

If her sister had noticed, perhaps the handsome Irishman truly was interested in her. A shiver of anticipation shot through her. He was a miner, so she didn't want to feel this way about him.

"Nettie, you are impossible. How you come up with these ideas I'll never understand. You should be writing those fanciful novels we read."

"Maybe I'll write one about a sister who gazes longingly at a handsome miner while denying she cares about him." With a laugh, she twirled away and out of pinching distance.

Stella called, "Stop right now or you'll find pebbles in your side of the bed tonight. Of course, as deeply as you sleep rocks wouldn't bother you."

Both girls were laughing as they reached their home.

Inside they found Lance sitting in the kitchen nursing a black eye and busted mouth.

Stella put her books down and hurried to her brother. "What happened to you?"

"Nothing." He turned away.

Mama met her gaze. "He won't say. Tore his best shirt too." Her mother's expression clearly conveyed worry.

Stella mouthed "You try" to her sister.

Nettie nodded. Her gentle ways often pried details out of their brother.

"Mama, I need your help with that dress I've been altering." Stella led her mother to the other part of the house.

She and her mother stayed in the girls' bedroom until she heard the front door slam.

Nettie slipped into the room. "He wouldn't say anything except that someone accused Papa of something he didn't do. I suspect this has to do with what Papa mentioned the other day after the cave in."

Mama wiped away a tear with her apron. "I'm so tired of these accusations."

Stella clasped her mother's hand. "Plural, Mama? Who's accusing Papa of anything?"

Their mother sat on the bed. "Did I say that? I must be upset." She peered down as she pleated her apron in her hands.

Sitting beside Mama, Stella gently lifted her mother's chin so their eyes met. "Explain, please. We aren't babies. You should tell us."

"I didn't want to worry you, but some people are accusing your father of causing the so-called accidents that have plagued the mine lately."

Nettie gasped. "That's ridiculous. Papa would never hurt anyone."

Mama nodded. "Don't you think I know that? But someone wants him to take the blame. He can't figure out who or why." She told them about the false covers on the vents.

Stella slid her arm around her mother's shoulders. "So that's why that young man fell yesterday and what Papa meant about the cave in not being an accident. But surely Mr. O'Neill doesn't agree or he wouldn't have come to get Papa last night."

"I suppose not, but who can say? When meanness like this starts, no one knows who to trust. Such goings on demoralize workers. Last week Juan Huerta refused to go down into the mine with Papa. Mr. O'Neill traded with Huerta and that's why he's on Papa's crew now."

Stella wondered who put Mr. Huerta up to wanting off the crew. Surely not Mr. O'Neill? No, she wouldn't consider him doing so unless she had proof.

She tugged on her mother's hand. "Why don't you go lie down and Nettie and I will finish supper?"

Her mother rose. "I need to stay busy or I'll worry even more. I've been a miner's wife for a quarter century and this is the first time I've had the fear of evil among us."

"Even when there were strikes back home?" Nettie asked.

Her mother touched each girl's face. "Home? Do you girls still think of England as home?"

The sisters exchanged worried glances.

Stella said, "No, Texas is my home."

"Me, too, Mama. I only meant our other home. Just a figure of speech." Nettie appeared ready to cry.

"You're good girls. Stella, perhaps you'd go find your brother and see he's all right. I'd hate for him to get into more trouble."

"I will. And then I'll box his ears for worrying you." She made a comical face and stood like a prizefighter.

Her silliness brought the desired smile to her mother's face. "Go on with you."

Stella left her home and peered around the town. The rows of small company-furnished homes had small dirt-packed yards. A few had straggly flowers planted near the door. More had small garden patches in back.

She missed the English gardens abundant with colorful blooms. She, Mama, and Nettie had tried to recreate one here. The weather was so different that many of the seeds they'd brought didn't do well. They'd been able to trade with neighbors, though, and even the small sampling of flowers at her home brought her pleasure.

Children played in the dirt street or front yards, but she didn't spot her brother. She strolled up and down the hill, searching for Lance. She spotted one of his friends but wouldn't embarrass her brother by asking about him.

After searching until she couldn't think where else to look, she met her father and Mr. O'Neill leaving the mine with other men as the night crew went inside. How odd it would be to work all night and try to sleep in the day. She supposed with the mine dark as pitch, once inside there was no difference. But sleeping in daytime with all the noise must be hard.

She walked to meet her father. "Hello, Papa."

"And what are you doing out at this time of day? Don't tell me your brother has gone off again?"

"Okay, I won't tell you." She looped her arm with his.

He pulled away. "Careful, dear, you'll soil your dress."

Mr. O'Neill walked beside her. "Shall I look for the lad?"

"Would you? I know he's embarrassed when I search for him. I don't want to add to his problems."

Papa asked, "What other problems?"

Instantly she regretted her choice of words. "I'll let Mama tell you."

He grabbed her shoulder and turned her toward him. "Tell me now, Stella Grace."

Heaving a sigh, she met her father's gaze. "He was in a fight but wouldn't explain. When Nettie tried to get him to talk, he rushed out of the house."

His face taught with anger and fatigue, Papa said, "More accusations, I suppose. You might as well know, there's talk I'm behind the so-called accidents that aren't accidental."

She touched his arm, hoping to reassure her father. "But we know they're lies, Papa. You would never do anything to hurt another person."

Some of the tenseness left his face. "Doesn't help your brother. Rumor says that's why he doesn't go into the mine, because I won't let him since I cause the problems. Has to be hard on the boy."

Mr. O'Neill clapped her father on the shoulder. "I'll find him and see if he'll talk to me. If not, at least I can send him home to you."

"Thanks, O'Neill. I appreciate your help."

Stella watched the handsome man she thought of as Finn even though she called him Mr. O'Neill. He strode swiftly to the wash area.

Her father caught her staring. "He's a good man. Sure glad he's here."

"Let's get you home, Papa, so you can rest until supper." She wished she'd invited Finn to eat with them. If he walked home with Lance, she would. If he even found Lance. If Lance would come home.

Chapter Six

Finn washed up as well as he could without bathing. He strolled across the town, back and forth. He'd almost given up finding the lad when he saw a hunched figure seated on a rock high on a ledge overlooking the company store.

Casually, he sauntered over and sat beside Lance. Muted light from the setting sun disguised the town's grubbiness. Instead, he looked out over the distant valleys and hills. "Kind of nice up here."

Lance refused to look at him. "There's nothing nice in this stinking town. I hate this place."

"Do you long for your home in England then?"

"I hated there too. We thought things would be better here, but they're worse. At least no one in England accused Papa of wrong doing."

"Who's accusing him here?" Finn idly observed a train's progress as it pulled coal cars from the mine and headed west and wondered how many of those miners filled each day.

Lance still wouldn't look up, and offered only a shrug. "Never mind. Don't think I don't know my family sent you." He glanced up. "I'll bet Stella asked you to come, didn't she?"

"No one asked me." He tilted Lance's chin up. "That's quite a black eye there and I imagine your lip hurts like hell. I hope the other guy looks as bad."

"Guys. And they don't. Tore my best shirt too. Mama was pretty mad."

This was bad news. Brutes tackling one small lad? "I see. They ganged up on you. How many?"

"What does it matter? No one can help me. I won't believe the lies about Papa. And I don't want to become a miner but there's nothing else, is there?"

Finn picked up a pebble and tossed it at a nearby boulder. "If you had a choice o' anything, what would you be?"

The boy grimaced, or as much as his battered face probably allowed. "A doctor. Isn't that a laugh?"

"Sounds like a good plan. There's always a need for doctors to heal the sick. Have you checked into what's involved getting into medical school?"

Lance pounded his knees with his upturned fists. "Why would I? We barely have enough to get by on. There's no money for university or my sisters would have gone. There's no money for anything."

"I know the feeling, lad. I grew up with far less than your family has. If 'tweren't for me brother in law, I don't know what would have happened to me family."

"I might have brothers in law some day, but they'll probably be miners. That won't help my sisters or me. Neither one wants to marry a miner. Um, no offense."

Finn chuckled. "None taken, but I'm thinking Llewellyn will not take the news well. He's that sure of your sister Stella."

"Him? She doesn't even like him. I mean, she doesn't dislike him exactly, but she doesn't think of him as a…a suitor."

"That's good news to me. But let's go back to your problems. See, sisters don't know that no one can fight your battles for you. They try to fix everything. Just smile and say thank you. Can you do that?"

"I don't think so. Stella and Nettie won't leave me alone. They want details of who says what and why. Honestly, I wish you'd talk to them instead of me. I mean, I'm glad you're talking to me, but I wish you'd also tell them I have to fight my own battles and live my own life."

"I'll try. I've only just convinced me own sister o' that, though, and I'm a lot older than you. With two sisters instead o' me one, I suspect you have another five or ten years o' meddlin' to deal with. And frankly, I suspect we're both stuck with our sisters meddlin' for life."

Lance frowned and appeared to study Finn. "You're not like the other miners I know."

"No? Every one o' is unique, don't you agree? You're not like me younger brother."

The boy reared back and stared at him. "You never mentioned you had a brother. You only said you had a sister."

Finn chuckled at the thought of his wild brother. "Because me brother is a pain in the arse. Always causing problems. Ran off and married when he wasn't much older than you to a girl barely your age. But he's shaping into a man now, mostly because o' me sister's husband."

"What's your sister like?"

"She has hair the same color as Stella's and a fiery temper to match. Her name is Cenora Rose and she truly believes every superstition she's ever heard."

"You like Stella because she reminds you of your family?"

"Lord, no. I swore I'd never be attracted to a redhead because of the temper that usually goes along with the hair color. Do something she thinks is wrong or fail to do something she things you ought, and a redhead lights into you. Many's the time I've received the sharp edge o' Cenora's tongue. Me sister is also kind, though. She's a loving wife and daughter and sister."

"Huh. The temper and sharp tongue sounds like Stella all right."

"Aye, but you know she loves you, lad, and would do anything for you. We're lucky, we are. Many's the man who has no one to care whether he lives or dies. You have two sisters and parents who want only the best for you. Which is why they don't want you to work the mines."

"Mr. O'Neill, do you like mining?"

Finn stared at the boy. "Are you daft? I hate it. And you should call me Finn for 'tis me name." He shrugged. "But here I am for a while, so I do me best at the job."

"Then you don't agree Papa's causing problems?"

How could he answer? "I suspect your father is the best man here. He's good to work for and 'tis glad I am to be on his crew. No man works harder than he does."

Lance smiled as broadly as a split lip allowed. "Thanks, Finn. That's what I believe, too. I don't know why people say otherwise."

"There're two possible reasons. One, whoever's causing trouble has to push the blame on someone else so the troublemaker looks innocent. Two, people are susceptible to suggestion. When this troublemaker points out your father was near when there were cave ins and other things like that, the suggestion sticks in their minds. They allow themselves to be manipulated."

"I'm glad you don't think Papa is guilty."

Finn didn't deny the statement for he was starting to think maybe Clayton was innocent. He wished he knew, but hadn't been able to prove anything. He stood, cursing the stiffness that had come on him while sitting on the rock. "Come on, we'd better start back. Your parents will worry and you'll miss your supper."

He was relieved when Lance joined him without protest.

Strolling back toward town, Lance said, "I like the way you talk. Do you miss Ireland?"

Did he? He didn't think so. "'Tis a beautiful land with green like no other place, but I have no wish to go back there. I like Texas."

"But not mining. So, what do you want to do?"

"I've a mind to raise horses on me own ranch. Takes money, same as medical school."

"So we're both out of luck."

"Mayhap for now, but not forever." Or at least he hoped not. "When you have a dream, you have to look for the opportunity to make it come true, then seize the chance when it comes."

They ambled until in sight of the Clayton home. A house before theirs, Finn stopped and motioned Lance to go on.

"You could come in for supper. Mama wouldn't mind and you could talk to Stella."

Finn shook his head. "Not this time. You'll need to face your parents and your sisters on your own. Explain without losing your temper and you'll be surprised. I'll wager your Da will back you."

He watched until Lance opened the door. The lad waved once before he went inside. Finn turned and headed toward the longhouse. Wouldn't he have loved to go inside with Lance and share supper there? Now he hoped he could find something to eat, for he was that famished.

Children's laughter rang out as they played games in the street. Some people set on steps enjoying the air that carried the odors from suppers prepared in each small home. Others strolled as he was doing. Several men had a game of horseshoes going.

Dusk had closed in and deep shadows fell across the way. Sky turned shades of purple edged in pink and gold at the horizon. At this time of day nature painted the world with a pleasing palette.

When he reached his bunk, James was munching an apple.

"You have supper with the Claytons?"

"I've had nothing since breakfast except a chunk o' bread."

The other man pulled an apple from under his pillow. "Have this then, because they've cleared away the food. You might be able to talk the cook out of something."

"I'm too tired. Thanks for this apple. I'll eat extra in the morning." He bit into the fruit and savored the juicy flavor. The long walk after his day's work had stripped the last of his strength. He barely had energy enough to shuck off his clothes.

This was no life. At least the married men had families to offer comfort and support and a wife to cuddle with at night. How did the single men keep going?

He didn't mind working from before dawn until after dark on the ranch, but he hated being underground. 'Twas not a fit place for a human, only for worms and moles and gophers. Plus the repetitive hacking at the coal wrecked his back and shoulders.

Solve this puzzle soon or go mad. Think of Lippincott's fine ranch, boyo. 'Tis going to be yours if you can ferret out the troublemakers.

He figured there were multiple problems at work. He no longer suspected Karpinski either. The man was full of dark looks but he worked hard as he played. That left Swensen and Hartford. Neither man was on his crew. Mayhap he could strike up a conversation with Hartford at dinner or breakfast.

Swensen was married and lived in one of the houses near Clayton. What excuse could he find to talk to Swensen? Didn't he have a son working in the mine? Yeah, a kid about the same age as Lance Clayton.

Hmm, that fact set him to thinking, but he'd have to work on that another time. His mind had given all he could for this day. He laid the apple core beside his boots and fell asleep.

When he woke the next morning, the apple core was gone. Worse, his knife was visible inside his boot. Last night, he'd carefully covered his boots to conceal his weapons as he did each time he undressed.

He checked around him, but others appeared engrossed in dressing and making their way to the dining hall. Quickly, he pulled on his clothes and then his boots. He knelt and looked under his bed. Sure enough, the apple core was there next to his concertina and duffle bag.

James, called to him, "Hey, come on if you want to make up for missing supper last night."

"Coming." Shoving his shirttail into his britches, he grabbed the core and tossed it in the rubbish bin as he followed James.

He longed for a hot bath and his own bed at the ranch. The only reason he slept soundly in this bunk with a thin, lumpy mattress was his complete exhaustion. One thing was for sure, he was building muscles in his arms that would help him later on the ranch. He hoped that'd be on *his* ranch.

In the dining hall, Finn loaded up on extra food. He had to pay for two meals, which irritated him. Arguing with the cashier that he'd missed supper was futile, so he gave up and concentrated on eating his fill.

"How'd you sleep?" he asked James.

"Like the dead. You?"

Finn nodded because he'd stuffed his mouth with food. He swallowed and peered around. "Wondered if you noticed anyone messing with our things."

A furrow appeared in James' brow. "What do you mean?"

"Someone had moved my clothes around and the apple core was way under the bunk."

James laughed. "Probably a rat."

Finn believed that, but he suspected the two-legged variety. "Have you seen them in the bunkhouse…um, longhouse?"

The Welshman gestured with a piece of bread. "Naw, but they're bound to be around when there's food to be had, even crumbs and apple cores."

"Guess you're right." But Finn wasn't convinced. He was certain a human had disturbed his clothes and boots while he slept and unknowingly kicked the apple remains. But who and to what end?

Damned if the culprit wasn't a brazen one to bother things only a couple of feet from his head. Had he gone through Finn's pockets? He was grateful he'd burned Farland's note. There was nothing to link him to the mine owner. But he'd kept the letter from Cenora and that linked him to McClintock Falls.

All day, thoughts circled in his mind about his quest. Although a number of odd things had occurred, he was still no closer to learning who plotted against Farland Coal Mine. He gave himself over to mining and worked fast enough to keep up with Council Clayton.

After work, he strode out of the tunnel with his crew. Council coughed a lot. Finn wondered how much longer the man could work at his current rate.

Aleski clapped Finn on the back. "You still unwilling to play cards with me?"

"Right you are. Minin' is the only stupid thing I do."

Aleski laughed, as did the other three.

Jose Garza said, "You're a smart man, O'Neill. The Pole, he will take your money if you let him."

Aleski said, "Aw, it's only the scrip. Worthless anyway."

Ulys Young nudged Aleski. "Not as much as you have. Most of us have lost a part of our pay to you at one time or another."

Aleski frowned. "You saying I cheat?"

Ulys held out a hand to signal protest. "As good a player as you has no need."

The Pole's frown disappeared. "This is what I always say. Everyone is good at something. I'm good at cards. They speak to me."

"What do they say?" Finn asked with a smile.

"You know that is not what I meant, but they do say 'there is the ace' or 'that man has the king.' Then I know how to manage my cards."

"Sure and I've known others with that ability, but I don't have it meself." Finn wasn't convinced Aleski didn't cheat. He won too often for the odds. Still, he might really be smart enough to keep track of the cards played and figure out who had what left in his hand. Was he also clever enough to stage "accidents" without detection?

Council, Ivan, and Ulys split off and walked toward the houses while Jose, Aleski, and Finn headed for the longhouse.

"I play the Solitaire," Jose said. "Then even when I lose, I keep my scrip."

"Smart." Finn said. "By now I'm so tired my brain is mush. Think I'll take a walk after supper and then turn in."

They reached the metal tubs and pump for washing up before they went inside to dine.

"Sí, tonight I am especially tired. I tried to keep up with you and Señor Clayton. You two will kill me, but we are sure to win the bonus this month."

"More scrip to waste at the store." Finn filled his plate with watery stew and took a chunk of thick bread.

Jose stayed beside him. "No, didn't you know the bonus is real money? If we win, I will give a part of my scrip to the boy who fell and broke his leg. He will be far behind by the time he can work again."

Finn couldn't hide his surprise. "Surely Farland will pay for all his care since he works and lives here."

Aleski laughed as they found seats at the long table. "Are you crazy? Farland will charge him for his stay at the hospital, the doctor's fees, nursing fee, and every meal he eats. He'll never get it all repaid."

Anger shot through Finn. "That's downright underhanded and makes me plenty mad. I'll donate some o' my pay also. And we will win the bonus."

The Pole nodded and forked up a bite of potato. "I believe so. I'll keep any cash we win but I'll donate my scrip winnings. After all, some belonged to the boy before he fell."

"That's good o' you both. Mayhap I'll take up a collection among the single men. Those who are married need every piece of worthless scrip they can get."

Aleski speared a bite of meat. "Isn't that the truth? When I've enough, I'll bring my woman here."

"Oh, didn't know you're married."

Aleski beamed. "Renia and my son Lucjan live with my parents near Warsaw. Since the Russians took over, my family has suffered. That's why I came to America, but we could scrape together only enough for one fare."

Jose nodded. "Sí, I came from South Texas. My wife waits with her mother until I send for her. Señor Farland said I can have the next house that comes available, and then Maria and my son and daughter can be with me."

"Sorry to hear you fellas have to live separate from your wives. No way for married folks to make do." And plenty of reason to take someone's payoff to cause trouble.

Finn thought about each of these two men. They both worked hard and he liked each man. He'd hate learning that one of them had set out to kill or maim other miners for extra money.

James sat across from Finn and glanced at Finn's plate. "I see you're making up for no supper last night."

Finn greeted him and continued eating. "I'm still a growing boy, you know."

James pretended to gaze at his stomach. "You keep eating like that and you'll be growing a paunch. Can't swing a pick if you're fat."

"Hard as we work, there's no chance o' that. I'm trying to keep me weight the same. If I lose pounds, I won't be able to work fast enough to win the bonus."

"Forget it, Irish. My crew's winning the bonus this month. Probably in the months to come as well."

"Guess we'll see this Friday, won't we?" Finn rose and walked to the dish bin positioned on a table near the door for the men to leave their dirty plates and cutlery. He walked outside and toward the rock where he'd seen Lance last evening.

He had to learn who was behind the mischief. No, this was too serious to be called that. Mick could have died. Other men had, yet someone or several men conspired for their own ends.

What was the goal? Did the conspirators want the mine to fail or to bring in a union? If he knew the answer, he'd know who to target for proof.

Chapter Seven

Stella set her cup down with a clunk. "Finn says this and Finn says that. I declare you are certainly taken with that man. You act as if he's the Oracle of the East."

Lance met her glare with one of his own. "I only mentioned him. It's not like I talk to that many people."

"You've talked of nothing else since he found you two evenings ago. I'm tired of hearing the man's name."

Her brother glanced at their father before directing his attention to her. "No wonder he said he'd sworn not to marry a woman with red hair like yours and his sister's." He appeared shocked he'd blurted that out but Papa laughed.

Stammering, he tried to cover his blunder, "I mean he said he likes you."

She rested both her palms on the table, her anger climbing. "Likes me, does he? But just the same vowed not to marry a woman like me? As if I'd want to marry a miner in the first place and him specifically."

Her brother leaned forward. "He don't plan to mine forever, Stella. He wants a ranch where he can raise horses. And he talks different than the others his age. He's more like Papa."

"Humph, he won't earn the money to buy a ranch while working here." Knowing he even wanted to was good news, but hopeless. She had no need of a dreamer; she wanted a man who made his dreams come true. Working for scrip would never buy anything worthwhile.

She reined in her thoughts and immediately guilt overwhelmed her. She'd vowed to be careful of her complaints for she didn't want even to appear she criticized Papa. He worked so hard to feed and clothe them. But darn it, she didn't want this life forever.

Lance hung his head. "Aw, I've made a mess of telling what he said. What he meant is that he didn't intend to, but he admires you."

Papa touched Lance's shoulder. "Stop while you're only a little behind, lad. You'd best let your sister mull this over in silence."

"Yes, sir, I see that now." He turned toward his father. "He also said you'd back me that day, Papa, and you did. Sorry I ran off like that."

"That's behind us now, son. Eat your dinner. Perhaps I should ask Finn to eat with us this Sunday." Papa's eyes twinkled with mischief.

Mama tried to hide a smile, but Nettie laughed openly.

Stella rose and carried her plate to the dishpan. "Thank you for thinking this is so humorous. Glad I could brighten your evening."

Mama said, "Now, Stella, we weren't laughing at you, but at the situation. Poor Mr. O'Neill is being talked about without being here to defend himself."

Stella stood at the dishpan, her chest heaving with tears she dared not shed. She couldn't say why Lance's talk had upset her so much. Normally she would have laughed it off.

But Finn O'Neill *was* different than the other miners. He shared her love of music, he was a hard worker, and now she learned he didn't plan to be a miner forever.

Stella spotted their dessert cooling beside the sink. She longed to throw the pie against the wall and wail at the hopelessness of their lives. Instead, she took a deep breath, forced a smile, and turned. "You're right, Mama. Shall I bring our pie to the table?"

Gathering the dessert pan and small plates, she set them beside her place. Her chest ached from suppressing her emotions but, as she often did, she pretended nothing was wrong. What purpose would upsetting her family serve?

Nettie rose. "I'll get the knife to cut the pie and refill everyone's cup while I'm up."

Dinner passed with chatter around her, but Stella only pretended to listen. She couldn't get Finn O'Neill out of her thoughts. Did he actually admire her? Would he be able to break free from mining and someday buy a ranch? For his sake, she hoped he would. For their sakes, she hoped she and her family would also.

***

Finn had a plan to determine who had poked around his clothes. To tempt the guilty person, he took out his sister's letter and read it at supper and then reread it before turning in. He pretended even more interest in her note than he had for by now he'd memorized the words.

That evening after everyone had turned in, Finn fought to remain awake while feigning sleep. He'd placed his clothes the usual way covering his boots. He was exhausted and couldn't last long without sleep. Whoever was creeping around must have the same problem and he didn't expect he'd have long to wait.

The longhouse filled with snores and deep breathing and a few men mumbled in their sleep. Finn didn't believe he snored, but he did what he hoped was a good imitation of deep breathing. Soon the rustling of someone approached.

He lay perfectly still until he heard the sneak beside him. Swiftly, he sat up and grabbed the meddler's arm.

Following a gasp, Jose whispered, "Aii, Señor O'Neill. I mean no harm."

He was stunned that the guilty person was his crew mate and a man he liked. Tugging the man's arm, Finn pulled him toward the door and outside. A bright moon shed light among the shadows. Noise from the night crew drifted up from across the ravine.

Though both men were barefoot and wore only their union suits, Finn tugged Jose far enough from the bunkhouse that they wouldn't be overheard if their exit had waked anyone. He released Jose and faced the man. "Why are you nosing around my things?"

"Someone tells me that you are spying for the Monticello Coal Mine owner. I don't believe this and we argue. He say if I check your things, I will find proof."

"What kind of proof? You think I would work so hard for a bonus if I was here for another mine company?"

"This is what I told this man, but he insisted. We wagered money, señor, and you know I need the cash for my Maria."

Finn's anger grew that someone took advantage of this man who so wanted his wife with him. "Who put you up to this, Jose? I want his name."

The other man shook his head. "I cannot say or he will be very angry with me and maybe he would not pay."

"If you don't say, I'll be angry with you." He tapped his chest. "You owe me the information, since you're the one prying into my things."

The other man shifted from one bare foot to the other, then raised a hand. "What you say is true. The man is Darius Hartford."

"He's in our longhouse. Why didn't he search himself?"

"Because he sleeps at the other end from us. My bed is just across the aisle from yours. He says I can search without being caught."

"Isn't he the one who's always talking up the unions?"

"Sí, that is him. Señor Farland cheats us in many ways, this is true. Hartford, he believes a union would help us. Perhaps he is right, but

I do not want this talk to cost me my job."

"Unions might help, but they also bring other problems. Why did Hartford pick you? Are you amigos?" Angry as he was at someone prying into his personal belongings, he knew how much Jose longed to have his wife with him. He directed his ire at Hartford for using this man so desperate for cash.

Jose shrugged. "He was hired when I was, so we were new together. But he has worked in a mine before in England. He gave me…what you call tips to help me."

"Look, man, I like you and trusted you because we work together on the same crew. Hartford is using you. Tell him he's wrong. I don't work for another mine company. This one is all I can manage."

"Por favor, I am sorry for my part. Perhaps he will agree I win the wager. It is for cash, not scrip and will help me save for Maria to come."

Finn's interest grew. "Real money? Where does he get cash?"

Jose shrugged again. "I don't know, but he has real coins."

"English?"

"No, American."

Finn wondered what that meant. Sure he had cash, but he hadn't been working in a mine before. "Don't tell him I caught you. But if he welshes on his bet, I'll talk to him."

"What means welshes? He is from England, not Wales."

"Means if he won't pay what he owes you." Finn clapped Jose on the back. "Let's get back and get some sleep."

They went back in and each went to his bunk.

James rolled over and scratched his stomach. "Where you been at this hour?"

Finn fell back on his bunk. He'd had enough of nosey people for one night. "Answering nature's call."

All the next day, Finn thought about Hartford. Was he the one causing problems? Accidents would pave the way for union organizers to gain a foothold by assuring miners that unions would insure safety precautions were observed.

But would they really be able to make a difference? Finn had no idea. How safe can any man be in a tunnel underground? He sure felt at risk every minute of his time there.

And he hadn't been able to get close to Johann Swensen. That man was one Farland suspected and someone Finn disliked. Fighting to be objective, he considered Hartford and Swensen side by side but reached no conclusion. Either man, or both, could be guilty.

The next morning at breakfast, he sat beside Hartford. "Mornin'. Lookin' forward to today."

The other man blinked in surprise and scooted a couple of inches away. "Yeah? Why?"

"My crew will be getting' closer to winnin' the month's bonus."

A furrow creased Hartford's brow. "What makes you think your bunch will win? Anything could happen today and tomorrow."

Finn raised his eyebrows. "Sounds like a threat, man. You have something planned to stop us?"

Hartford held up both hands. "Whoa, didn't mean anything like that. But you can never tell in this business. If we had a union, they'd be watching to see our work place was safer."

"You sound like a man who's had experience with a union. You in one where you worked before this?"

Hartford nodded. "Matter of fact I was. They took care of us miners, too."

"Why'd you leave there then?"

"I wanted to come to America. Intended to work in Virginia, but Farland made me an offer. Heard about the Wild West and thought I'd check out Texas."

"What's your opinion?"

He paused as if thinking over his answer. "Don't mind the state, but there're too many accidents happening. We need the union to protect us."

"You think the problem is all Farland's negligence?"

Hartford took a bite of biscuit and nodded while he chewed. "I heard talk against Clayton, but don't much believe he'd plan anything like the cave in or explosion or that kid falling. If anyone besides Farland is guilty, Clayton isn't the one."

"I agree. But Farland wouldn't cause the problems in his own mine. I figure someone else is trying to drive him out o' business."

"Out of business? I hadn't thought of that, but now that you mention the possibility the idea makes sense. Why else would anyone cause these problems? Makes me want to quit."

Finn pointed his fork at Hartford. "Exactly. If we all get spooked and quit, where does that leave Farland? Plus, look at how much all the so-called accidents have slowed production."

"I see what you're saying. Union would still help us, but

someone's playing dirty. If I find out who, I'll beat the black-hearted devil half to death before I turn him in to Farland."

"Sounds right. Let's hope we both avoid falling prey to the plot of o' whoever's causing the troubles."

He thought Hartford spoke truthfully to a point. He'd wager the union organizers were paying the man to talk up their cause. Still, Finn didn't believe Hartford had caused any of the problems that resulted in death and injury. So, that crossed him off the list of suspects.

Finn grabbed extra bread for his lunch pail and filled his galvanized canteen with water. Recalling the bountiful meals with his sister and brother in law, he gave thanks he wasn't stuck here in Lignite permanently. Some of the men he'd met here would work in the mine as long as they lived, and their lives were bound to be cut short either by accident or disease.

At work during the morning, Council sent him several odd glances. At lunch, Finn stood beside him while he ate. There was nowhere to sit and the floor carried the ever present water.

"You upset with me?" he asked the crew chief.

Council appeared surprised. "Not at all. Looks like we'll make the bonus if we keep up this rate through tomorrow."

"Hope so. Aleski and Jose want to bring their wives here and need the money."

"Didn't know that. Thanks for telling me." Council sent him a strange glance. "You thought of marrying anytime soon?"

Finn wondered why the crew chief would ask such a personal question. "Someday, but I don't have enough money saved yet."

"Good planning. You have a girl in mind?" Council took a bite of his bread and cheese rather than meet his gaze.

He paused and stared at the crew chief. "Are you asking me for a particular reason?"

Council chuckled. "No, just curious. You seem driven to work as hard as your body will stand. I wondered if you had a reason."

This was a peculiar conversation and not typical for his crew chief. "I always give my best at whatever I'm doing. This is no different."

"Glad to hear it. Say, Grace and I would like for you to eat with us Sunday."

The invitation lightened his mood and pleasure radiated to his chest. "Sure and I'll look forward to then. 'Tis pleasant to sit with a family in a real home."

His answer appeared to please Council. "Bring your concertina.

We'll have music to cheer us. If we win that bonus, we'll have cause to celebrate."

"Aye, a ceilidh we'll have. That's Irish for a party with music and dancing. And I'm thinking we'll win this month."

That evening on his walk through town after supper, he saw Lance Clayton being accosted by three boys. The two Swensen boys and another he didn't know had Lance trapped against the side of the company store.

Finn ambled over as if unaware what was going on. "Hey, Lance, you're just the man I wanted to see."

The three ruffians scowled, but appeared nervous. Mayhap they feared what he'd do to them for ganging up on someone. Or, mayhap they didn't want their parents to know about their bullying.

He stepped by the boys and clapped Lance on the back. "Could I take you away from your friends to ask your help with something?"

Relief flooded the boy's face and he retrieved a package at his feet. "Sure, Finn."

When they were away from the other three boys, Finn asked, "Those the ones who attacked you before?"

Lance slid the package under his arm and stuffed his hands in his pants pockets. "Yeah. I try to avoid them but they were waiting for me when I came out of the store on Mama's errand. Thanks for getting me away without a fuss. I'm not a coward, but I can't beat three at once."

"Especially when two of them are larger than you. I recognize the Swensens, but who was the third one?"

Lance grimaced, or as much as he probably could with his split lip. "Vincent Evans. Those three work in the mines and think I should too. Plus when we were in school together, I did better than they did and that made them mad at me."

"Bullies always hate someone who does better than they're willing to work for."

"They call me a lazy coward, know-it-all teacher's pet, and a Mama's boy. I know I should work with Papa, but I don't want that life and he says I don't have to. Since we talked about medical school, I can't think of anything else."

"Stand your ground. You'll find a way eventually." Finn hoped he wasn't giving the boy false hope. He also hoped he hadn't set himself up for the same.

Lance peered up at him. "Did you really want to ask me

something?"

"Aye, I plan to ask your sister to go for a walk. If she'll go, I thought I'd take her up to that rock where you hang out. Nice view up there. Figure that's your special place, so thought I should clear with you first."

"Really? Well, sure. That's real nice of you. You sweet on her?"

That was an understatement. He dreamed of her at night and thought of her during the day. "If I am, would that be all right with you?"

"Yeah. She needs something special to happen. All she does is teach school and help Mama. I mean, Mr. Llewellyn comes by, but she won't go out with him. He still comes to see her, though."

And would hate Finn if she went for a walk with him. "She might not go out with me either, but I'll ask her anyway."

"Jonas Evans used to ask her out, but she turned him down so much he don't ask anymore. But he still watches her in church."

They reached the Clayton home and paused at the road. "Could be Llewellyn scared him off. Tried to warn me, but I told him she was the only one who could tell me she wasn't interested."

Lance nodded toward the house. "You coming in? You could talk to Stella?"

"No, I'll wait for another day when I've cleaned up before I call on her. Best not to mention this conversation."

Finn watched while Lance hurried into his home then he turned and walked to the longhouse. So, Swensen's boys were the ones who beat up Lance? He wondered if that was due to talk they'd heard from their father. Did Johann Swensen believe Clayton caused the disasters in the mine, or did he want others to believe that?

Chapter Eight

Friday evening, Stella laughed as her father regaled them with news of his crew winning the month's bonus. Heaven knew lately there few enough causes for laughter. She answered a firm knock on the door and was surprised to see Finn O'Neill standing on the porch.

He wore clean clothes and a smile. The nerve of him, smiling at her when he didn't like her red hair and thought her temper fiery. She should slam the door in his face but that would only add fuel to his opinion.

"Did you want to see Papa?" Her voice carried frost, but she was still angry.

Apparently undaunted, his smile widened and his dark eyes twinkled. "I came to ask you for a walk."

"A-A walk?" She took a deep breath. Don't stutter instead of answering. She intended to refuse him with a sharp remark, but she heard herself say, "I'll get my shawl and tell Mama where I'm going."

Some refusal. Instead, she was giddy as one of her giggling students. She left the door ajar while she hurried to grab her shawl. "Mama, I'm going for a walk with Mr. O'Neill."

Mama's eyes widened, but she only nodded. Beside Mama, Nettie grinned from ear to ear. She could imagine Nettie would be full of teasing when she returned.

Breathless in her haste before one of her family made a comment, Stella closed the door behind her. She should have asked him in instead of leaving him standing on the porch but she'd been so flustered. Too late now.

He offered his arm, and she laid her hand there, pleased he had manners. They stepped off the porch together and proceeded through town.

Still, she hadn't recovered from the sting of his remarks to Lance. "I'm surprised you'd ask me to walk with you."

"Why is that? Surely you realize I can't keep me eyes off o' you when you're near."

"You told Lance you vowed never to go near a woman who had

red hair and a quick temper."

He appeared puzzled. "True, though I should not have told your brother. I didn't want to find you or any other woman here in Lignite attractive, but I can't help meself."

"You make me sound like a case of influenza."

His quick laugh startled her. "Did I? Does a man ask influenza out for a walk? 'Tis true me sister has hair like yours and a fiery temper to match. Believe me, other than those two things, you're nothing alike. And I'll warn you that what I feel for you is not brotherly."

"Oh, I see." She felt the heat of a blush on her cheeks and thought she'd best change tactics. "Tell me about your family. What's this sister's name?"

He nodded to someone they passed. "Cenora Rose. She's about your age or what I guess your age to be. She and her husband live on a ranch. Me younger brother is named after me dad, Brendan Sean O'Neill. We call him Mac, which you probably know is Irish for 'son of'."

"Your sister's name is lovely and I've not heard the name Cenora before. I do know about Mac's meaning. Is your Mac a rancher too?"

He made a tusking sound. "I wish 'twere so but he's not overfond o' work is that boyo. He's had a bit o' trouble finding his way. Last summer he married a girl too young to wed. Not in years exactly, although she's only Lance's age, but she's very childish. They live in a caravan beside me parents."

"A caravan? How interesting. Tell me about your parents." She had no idea where they were headed, but he appeared to have a destination in mind.

"Ma and Da live in a sweet little house me brother in law bought them. They're in the town o' McClintock Falls, or at the edge, but have a cow and chickens and a large garden plot. 'Tis in heaven they are for that's all they've wanted since we lost our place in Ireland."

She sent him what she intended as a sympathetic glance. "I'm sorry they lost the place they loved in Ireland."

"The one they have now is far better than the one they lost so 'tall worked out for the best. Me sister is happy and expecting a babe soon. Vourneen won't be far behind her. Me parents are happier than they've ever been."

"That's wonderful. And you want to live near them. If only Papa would look for some other work before the mine kills him, perhaps we could find a place where my family could live near one another. You already know I don't want Lance forced into that life."

He turned her to look out over the town. "Here is what I wanted you to see."

"I had no idea the view was so lovely up here. Thank you for bringing me."

He pulled a large piece of cloth from his jacket pocket and spread the fabric on a boulder. Then, he bowed elegantly. "Your seat, me lady."

She couldn't suppress a smile as she sat carefully. "Thank you, kind sir."

He took a place beside her. "Lignite looks best from up here. At this time o' day, the light hides the grubbiness I find oppressive."

She peered at him. "You puzzle me."

Surprise spread across his handsome face. "Me? Why?"

"You aren't like the other miners. Why are you here?"

"I'll tell you that story another time, but I'll not be a miner forever. Someday I'll own me own ranch."

Another dreamer? Bitterness overtook her. "You won't get the money working for scrip."

"Too true." He took her hand. "Just the same, I'll have me own place someday soon."

She wanted to yell at him, but held her voice under control. "How, Mr. O'Neill? How can you ever earn enough while working in Lignite?"

His fingers twined with hers. "Please, call me Finn, will you?"

Frustration tinged her voice, but she was helpless to soften her words. "All right, Finn. You can call me Stella. But you still haven't answered my question. How can you work here and even hope to own a ranch?"

"You'll have to trust me, Stella." He brushed a stray curl from her face.

She gave up on his dreams to ask a question of uppermost importance. "Do you think Papa is to blame for the trouble at the mine?"

"What I believe is that whoever is causing the trouble wants your father to look guilty, maybe even be arrested or injured."

She exhaled a whoosh of breath. "Thank you for not believing those horrid rumors."

He caressed her cheek with his free hand. "Do you think we could walk out together steadily, Stella?" His voice was soft and his touch gentle.

Her discouragement lessened. He appeared to be a fine man even if he was a dreamer. Could she consider letting him court her? She tried to turn away but his gaze mesmerized her.

"I think so."

He leaned forward and brushed his lips across hers, soft as a feather's touch. Her first kiss lasted only a second but the effect was magical. She wished he'd repeat the stirring contact and linger.

He tilted her chin upward. "Seems a shame to waste time with a beautiful woman on this lovely evening with all this talking."

She knew the kiss was coming and could only lean toward him. His lips were soft at first but increased in pressure. As if by their own volition, her arms slid around him.

By the time he broke the kiss, she was breathless. He kissed her brow, her eyes, and along her jaw before returning to her eager lips. What had come over her that she permitted such freedom? Not only permitted, but responded with kind.

She melted against him as his tongue slid along her lips, pressing the seam until she opened for him. Heavens above, she'd never imagined such a way to kiss. She'd never have imagined the warmth pooling in her private parts or the way her heart pounded so hard she feared it would leap from her chest.

He broke their embrace but cradled her head against his shoulder. "I had no intention o' taking such liberties, Stella. I only wanted to learn if you could ever return my feelings."

And she had practically attacked the man. "You learned that all right. I hope you don't think less of me for kissing you back."

"I'd have been torn to bits if you hadn't. What chance would I have had to court you if you didn't like kissing me?"

She raised her head and touched his jaw. "C-Court me? Finn, don't say things like that unless you mean them."

He stood and pulled her to her feet. "If you say I can come courting, then 'tis a lucky man I am, Stella Clayton."

Suddenly uncustomary shyness overwhelmed her. "Y-Yes, you can come calling."

He lifted her and twirled her around.

She laughed, her joy bubbling up from deep inside her. "Put me down before we tumble down the hill."

"Aye, and that would change our plans." After folding up the cloth, he stuffed it into his jacket pocket.

He guided her away from their perch on the boulder. "I'd best get you home before your father comes looking for us with his shotgun."

She couldn't suppress her laughter. "He doesn't own a gun. He'd be more apt to wait up and give us a scolding. I suppose we had better get back though because you have to work early tomorrow."

He caught her when she would have turned her ankle on loose rocks. "Aye, but I'm invited for dinner on Sunday. If 'tis all right, I'll be along to walk you to church."

So, he was a church going man. That added to her joy. "Are you sure? Doing so will start talk about us."

"As long as none o' the talk damages your reputation, I care not. Mayhap you'd walk to Spencer with me after lunch on Sunday. Someone from your family can accompany us so there won't be any rough talk."

He was considerate and kind. She wanted him to be the one to show her new places. Her face heated at all the new things he could teach her. Things she shouldn't think about now.

To cover her distraction, she said, "I'd like that. I've never been there."

He stared at her with surprise etched on his face. "What? Never? In a year you've not left Lignite?"

Clearly he didn't quite understand their position. "We have *no* cash, Finn. Nothing but scrip, so there's no point going to see things we can't have."

"Your father's winnings? 'Tis not much, 'tis true. My share was a dollar, but his was three. And surely he's won other months."

She nodded. "But that money goes straight into the bank in case Papa is injured and can't work. As far as Nettie, Lance, and I are concerned, we're penniless."

His expression changed to somber, and he nodded. "Sure and I can understand that, for there were many years when I had naught. 'Tis another tale for another time."

She waved at Mr. and Mrs. Young as they passed that house. "I want to know more about you and your family. You already know mine."

"Not everything. For I don't know why your father became a miner or where he met your mother or where you were born or what you thought of traveling here."

"You'll find none of that is interesting." She was sad to notice they'd reached her house.

"Mayhap 'twill be to me. I'll enjoy learning more about you on our future walks." He led her up the steps but immediately stepped away.

"I'll not steal a goodnight kiss because your neighbors are

watching. I bid you goodnight with thanks for walking out with me."

She smiled at him and knew her heart's longing must be in her eyes. "Goodnight, Finn."

He touched his fingers to his forehead as if tipping a hat. "I'll see you Sunday."

Chapter Nine

Finn strolled toward the infirmary to visit Mick. When he arrived, Mick was propped up on three pillows. A broad smile split his face when he spotted Finn.

Finn sat in the chair beside his bed. "You seem in better spirits, lad."

"Some of the guys have been by and left me part of their paycheck. Karpinski gave me several times as much as I lost to him. They all said it was your idea. I owe you a lot of thanks."

He handed over a handful of his worthless scrip. "Here's more for your collection."

Mick stuffed the paper into a bag "I can't thank you enough. I was worried, for the bills are mounting. Doc says I won't be able to work for three months or more."

"Can you read?"

"Slowly, but I'd welcome some kind of book. I've nothing but time."

"I keep one with me and I'll bring it to you tomorrow. Mayhap others have one they'll loan you."

Mick asked, "Has anyone found out who covered the hole with tarp?"

"No, but many of us would like to know the answer to that question."

"I think it was Clayton. He has the knowledge."

"You're wrong there. He helped me find the others and remove the tarp. If you'd seen how upset he was, you'd know he wasn't acting. He swore to find out who was guilty and do him damage before he threw him down one of the holes."

Mick relaxed against his pillows. "That's a relief. I hated thinking that because his wife comes to visit and brings me little treats. Still and all, I'd sure like to see whoever did cause my fall go to jail."

"Depending on who learns the identity of the swine who caused your accident, he may not live to go to jail. Many o' the men have sworn to throw him down one o' the holes."

"I can't say I'd wish that for him exactly, but I'd sure like to see the man who put me here caught and punished."

"Me, too, lad. Me too. Well, I'll bring you a book when I come again. Take care."

Finn left and strolled back to the bunkhouse. By now, some of the men were already in bed. A few played cards with Aleski. Where did the man get his energy to stay up late playing poker when he worked hard for long hours?

James appeared beside him and sat on his own bunk. His face conveyed anger. "Saw you walking with Stella Clayton."

Finn sat on his bunk and faced James. "Yes, we walked for a while. I value your friendship, James, and hope this doesn't come between us."

The other man laughed, but the mirth didn't reach his eyes. "Sure, she made her choice. There are other women in town."

Relief spread through Finn in spite of James's half-hearted attempt. "Thanks for taking that attitude. 'Tis pointless to argue."

"Righto. You go see Mick?"

Finn nodded, eager to change the subject. "He's that happy many o' the men have given him part o' their scrip. Aleski gave Mick several times what he'd lost."

Before James could reply, a man Finn didn't' recognize opened the door. "Fire! The store's on fire! Everyone out to help."

Pandemonium spread as men who'd turned in scrambled into their clothes. Others rushed out toward the company store. Flames shot up from the store's roof and smoke billowed upward.

Men came from all over town. The company fire pumper wagon arrived to direct water to the center of the flames. Bucket brigades formed to wet down the untouched portion of the building. Where all the buckets had been stored, he had no idea.

Finn joined a line formed at the fire's edge. Heat pushed against him in waves, as he was the second nearest the flames. He thought they were wasting time, for a hundred buckets of water had no chance of dousing this fire.

This had to be another disaster orchestrated against Farland. When he and Stella had been on the hill above the store, there was no sign of smoke. Someone deliberately set this tonight after he and Stella left. Wouldn't they have seen anyone sneaking around?

He kept passing the pails to the man in front of him. Mayhap working with the firemen, their efforts would make a difference. At least they should do their best with the resources at hand.

The fire chief shouted to keep the fire from spreading. The line moved to wet down the building at the edge of the fire. Roasting temperatures radiated toward the men. Popping of bottles and cans exploding sounded like guns.

Continuing to pass buckets, Finn shouted at the nearest fireman, "Where are the explosives and ammunition kept?"

Horror passed across the man's face. He pointed at the opposite end of the store. "Heat from the fire could set off the explosives. If the flames pass the door there, draw back."

Finn nodded.

The pump truck ran out of water and had to hurry back to the garage to refill. In their absence, fingers of fire reached for fresh wood. Embers of red and black drifted through the air, threatening to spread the flames to other buildings. Wetted down by the water hose, the new wood smoked but then soon caught. Someone brought ladders to enable the men to take the brigade up rungs to climb toward the roof.

Soon, the ladder had to be moved to keep the men on it from being burned. By the time the truck returned, the fire was roaring. Though the firemen sprayed water, the fire chief directed the others to move back by the longhouses.

Finn joined his mates beside their longhouse. Men from town stood nearby, watching the destruction of their only source of staples. The murmur of angry and worried voices reached him.

What would the miners and their families do without the store? This was payday, so most wives probably shopped on Saturday. What would people eat until the store was repaired and restocked?

Once again, guilt of failure engulfed Finn. He hadn't discovered who was behind this crime spree? Why hadn't he figured this out?

This time, Farland was sure to fire him and he couldn't say he blamed the man. What would that do to his chance to have his ranch? And what else would happen to the miners?

Dear Lord, help me. Not just for me, but to protect those who will suffer from the villainous actions of whoever is doing this.

Council edged toward him. "Stella said you two walked above the store. Did you see anyone around?"

"Nothing out of the ordinary, but we weren't looking for anything. I took her up there because the town looks almost nice at sunset. If someone were up against the hill, he would be out o' sight from above."

Worry shadowed the other man's face. "Suppose I'll be blamed for this."

"Surely not. You were at home, weren't you?"

"With only my family as witness to that, so who's to believe me?"

Finn wanted to reassure his crew chief, but the man spoke the truth. Rumors are impossible to combat.

A man pointed his way and yelled, "There they are. Get them."

Another said, "I saw this one and Clayton's daughter walk from the store this very evening."

Finn edged backward as angry men advanced on him and Council. He held up his hand to stop them. "We weren't walking from the store, but above it. There's a group o' boulders up there where you can look out over the town and the land around."

The first man advanced. "And did you throw a fire bomb down from there?"

"No, are you crazy? Why would we do that?"

The second said, "They're in this together. Let's get 'em."

Council stepped in front of Finn. "The man is innocent, and so is my daughter and myself. You're looking in the wrong place."

Aleski and Jose stood by Council and Finn.

Aleski raised his arms and yelled. "This must stop now. These men are guilty of nothing but hard work. I work beside them every day. If they were bent on destruction, why would they work harder than anyone here? Go home or go stare at the fire, but leave my friends alone."

Three of Aleski's fierce-looking card-playing companions joined him. Crew members Ivan Gretsky and Ulys Young came to stand with them. Soot, ash, and sweat stained their faces.

Ulys shouted, "O'Neill speaks the truth. He and Miss Clayton passed by my house carrying nothing and returned the same way a short time later. They were walking proper and doing nothing they shouldn't. Think, men. If you were walking with a woman as beautiful as the teacher, would you have destruction on your mind?"

A couple of the men chuckled. Others hooted and sent knowing looks Finn's way. He didn't like the inference, but he wasn't arguing if the mob quieted and left them alone.

The first man glared at him. "Someone started that fire."

Finn met his gaze. "You're right, but it wasn't me and it wasn't Miss Clayton or her father here. You need to look elsewhere."

The second man touched the arm of the first. "Guess we got carried away. Come on, Sylvester."

People turned their focus back to the fire and left Finn and Council with their defenders.

"Thank you. You've made me proud and humbled with your show of support." Council shook each man's hand.

Finn looked each man in the face by turn as he shook his hand. "Thank you. You saved our necks. 'Tis proud I am to know you."

By midnight, the men dispersed while firemen continued to battle the blaze. Finn and his longhouse mates went to bed. He wondered where James had been. He appeared only as dirty as he had before they rushed out earlier.

Saturday morning, they learned the fire had burned for hours, but firemen prevented it reaching the explosives or spreading to other buildings. Smoke still drifted upward from the charred wood. Firemen stood guard, monitoring the site and watching for hot spots reigniting.

Finn followed his crew mates into the mine. The short night left him tired, but he worked as hard as his muscles allowed. This first day of October, he wanted to get a good start on this month's bonus.

Although he hoped he wouldn't be here all month, he couldn't say he'd solved anything. All he'd done was cross off a few names. Farland would want more, especially now that his store had burned.

At the noon break, Finn pulled off a chunk of his bread. "Thanks again for supporting me last night. Your defense meant a lot to me and probably saved my neck."

Council nodded. "Same goes for me, but double because my daughter was mentioned. I've heard the rumors about my involvement in the accidents here. I hope you know those are lies. Those of you with children can understand how upset I was to hear my daughter's name mentioned because of me."

Aleski clapped Council on the back. "We know the rumors aren't true. We've been with you when the cave ins happened. We'd know if you had caused them."

Council put away his lunch remains. "Then let's get to work and win the October bonus."

When they left work at six, a small man with thinning brown hair stood waiting. He singled out Finn. "Mr. Farland wants to talk to you about last night's fire."

Council asked, "Shall I come with you?"

The man shook his head. "Only O'Neill."

"Thanks. I've done nothing wrong and I'll see him on my own." Finn met Council's gaze. "If you hear I'm in jail, though, I'd appreciate you speaking up for me."

Finn followed the man who hadn't bothered to introduce himself. When they climbed to the top of the hill, they entered the mine offices. They stopped in front of a door with Farland's name in large gold letters.

After knocking, Finn went inside and closed the door behind him. He braced himself for the chewing out he figured was coming.

Farland glanced up from his desk. "What do you have to say for yourself?"

"I've nothing to say except 'tis sorry I am your store burned."

The man leaned back in his chair. "I heard you might have set the blaze."

"You know that isn't true, but I was accused last night until my mates defended me."

"I hired you to find out who's causing this trouble. Instead of doing what you were tasked with, more trouble has come. Explain yourself."

Finn nodded. "I've tried to find who's guilty. I've crossed several men off the list, but haven't found the guilty one."

"Who've you crossed off?"

"Council Clayton and Aleski Karpinski and Darius Hartford are not involved. Although Hartford talks up the union whenever anyone will listen, he wouldn't cause trouble."

"Didn't know about Hartford. Don't want unions messing with my mine."

"You have a problem then."

"What do you mean by that?"

"You aren't being fair to the men and their families. Prices at the store are too high. They can't go elsewhere, so are forced to hand over their scrip."

The owner's face turned red. "You have a nerve. I make an effort to have something of everything in that store. Not that it makes any difference now that it's destroyed."

Finn shrugged and continued to meet Farland's eyes. "You asked."

Farland appeared to calm slightly. "So I did. What about Swensen?"

"I don't like the man or his sons, but haven't been able to find out much about him."

"You're too cozy with Clayton. Heard you're seeing his daughter."

"And if I am?"

"Nothing, just seems you need to be spending all your effort finding out who's causing this trouble."

"Someone had covered the vent holes with tarp and shoveled dirt on them and removed the warning poles. At night, you couldn't tell they were there and a young man from my bunk…longhouse stepped through one. He could o' died, and his leg is broken."

Farland gave a dismissive wave. "I know about Gallagher's leg. Didn't know about the tarp though. Another incident to worry me."

"Clayton helped me find the other vent holes. His reaction was genuine disgust that anyone would be so evil."

"Harrumph, you're sweet on his daughter, so of course you'd say that. We'll see how you like working for Swensen. His crew can use a boost. Never come close to the output of Clayton's crew."

Finn was distressed by the news, but he'd hired on to do a job he'd yet to accomplish. "Clayton works harder than anyone on his crew even though we're younger. We all work harder trying to match him. But whatever you say."

"Damn right what I say goes. Monday, you report to Swensen. I've my hands full with the store burning." He tugged at his ridiculous mustache. "What am I to do?"

"Mayhap you can make arrangements with the stores in Spencer to take the scrip and you could promise to redeem the paper until the store is rebuilt."

Farland frowned and curled the ends of his mustache. "I'll lose a lot of money."

Finn was disgusted by the selfish man not considering the many people in his town. "Miners and their families have to eat. How else will they be able to buy what they need to survive?"

Farland pointed at him. "You'd better come through fast, O'Neill. Otherwise, you're out of here and I'll tell Uncle Victor to forget helping you buy that ranch."

"Yes, sir." Finn left the office and trudged down the hill to the longhouse. His dressing down had probably caused him to miss dinner. He hoped James had another spare apple.

Chapter Ten

Stella took special care getting dressed for church. She had only three dresses, and her best was a green foulard with lace at the throat. The ribbon Finn had given her matched the shade. She knew the garment's color complimented her hair and skin.

Would he still come to walk her to church? Her pulse raced at the memory of his kiss. She touched her lips, reliving the touch of Finn's mouth on hers.

"You're daydreaming again." Nettie nudged her.

She turned to face her sister. "What if I am?"

"I'm glad you have a beau, Stella. You deserve special treatment."

"No more than you. But I was just wondering if he'd really show up to walk me to church. Words are easy. Actions are harder."

A rap on the front door sent her rushing. Lance beat her there and invited Finn inside.

Adjusting her hat, she walked toward him. "I'm ready."

"You look lovely, but I wanted a word with your father."

She wondered what he wanted to say to Papa. Surely he wasn't going to ask for her hand. Not that she would mind if he truly planned to leave mining.

Papa stepped from his bedroom. "Here I am. What came of your summons?"

"Farland is transferring me to Johann Swensen's crew starting tomorrow."

Of all the things, that was the last she expected. Did that mean he'd stop coming around to see her?

Papa said, "That's bad news. I've enjoyed having you on the crew with me. You're a hard worker and smart as well as easy to get along with. The men will miss you."

"And I'll miss your crew, but I'm lucky not to be fired with all the talk."

"Does Farland believe you or I are guilty of the fire?"

Finn shook his head and stared at the floor. "Apparently not, but he said I was too comfortable working for you. He said Swensen's crew needs a hard worker, whatever that means."

Papa chuckled. "Swensen is always at the bottom of production. I've wondered why he hasn't been replaced as crew chief by now."

"Well, I don't like the change but have no choice. We'd best get on our way, but I wanted to let you know in case you run into him at church."

Papa clapped him on the shoulder. "Thanks."

Finn offered Stella his arm and she smiled her thanks. They had plenty of time to walk to the small church, but she was happy they didn't have to hurry. She'd liked their walk Friday night and wanted to stroll with him today.

The rest of her family followed them so they were all in a group. She was disappointed they would hear anything she said to Finn.

"Papa said people accused us of setting the fire."

"As upsetting as the charge was, others defended us. 'Tis grateful I am the Youngs saw us walking both ways and he spoke up."

"I wish the person doing these things would be found and all these rumors would die forever."

"Yes, 'tis what I want too. I can't figure out who's behind the trouble."

"Why would you?"

"I don't want anyone else hurt. Mick Gallagher could have died. As it is, he's in a lot o' pain and will miss months o' work. I understand that men have died in the cave ins. I've wracked me brain about who might be causing all this."

From behind them, Papa said, "So have I with no solution. Someone has it in for me, that's for certain."

"Mayhap because you so often win the bonus. Would that cause a man to go off the deep end and kill others?"

Papa sounded angry, "Small reason to cause the death of innocent men. I've considered everything I can think of, but can't figure out what's going on here."

Beside her, Finn said, "Farland should learn who's guilty. Right now, he has his hands full with the store's loss."

They reached the small white church with a steeple. Stella and Finn garnered some stares. Several women looked their way and nudged one another or put their heads together whispering. Worrying, she hoped he wasn't so embarrassed he decided not to come with her again.

When she gazed into his face, though, she saw his eyes twinkling and a broad smile on his face.

"Don't fash yourself, lass. Our walking together gives the gossips something to talk about. 'Tis harmless."

She exhaled a large sigh. "Glad you think so, because there's no way to prevent human nature."

Finn sat beside Stella on the pew her family chose. The church service was not so nice as the one in McClintock Falls, but 'twasn't bad since he had Stella beside him. The minister was an older man who pounded the lectern as he spoke. He must be what Finn had heard called a "fire and brimstone" preacher because he sermon carried nothing hopeful or cheerful to say.

There was no choir, but the congregation sang out on the hymns. Finn thought the Clayton family voices blended so well they carried over the others. He was pleased to join with them.

At the end of the service, the preacher read a note. "Mr. Farland had written to let you know that he's arranged for the mercantile and butcher in Spencer to accept your scrip until the store here is reopened."

After the service, they hurried to the Clayton home rather than linger to speak to others.

Later, Finn rubbed his stomach. "The stew was just what I needed. And the bread was the best I've had since the last time I was here."

Nettie smiled mischievously. "Stella baked it, same as last time."

Mrs. Clayton brought a pie to the table and commenced slicing it. "I hope you like vinegar pie, Mr. O'Neill. What with the store burning, this is all I could make with what I had on hand."

"Mrs. Clayton, you're a wonderful cook, so 'tis sure I am the pie will be delicious. 'Tis gracious you've been to have me in your home. Please, ma'am, call me Finn, and I ask the same o' all your family."

Appearing flustered, she smiled. "Well, I suppose I can."

Council asked, "I'm wondering who Farland will send to my crew from Swensen's. Did he give you a clue?"

"None. And believe me, the man was in no mood for questions. 'Tis lucky I am he didn't fire me."

Stella gazed at him, an unreadable expression on her face. If he guessed, she was wishing he had been fired so he'd do something besides mining. He couldn't quit yet, though, or he wouldn't get his loan. He prayed Lippincott's ranch hadn't been sold to someone else.

After their meal, Mrs. Clayton waved away her daughters' help. "You young people go ahead and get on to Spencer. Lance, you have my list. See you don't add anything else."

Each of the girls carried a medium-sized basket and Lance lugged a large one.

Council walked them to the door. He handed one of his dollars to each of his children. They stared at him then at the money then back to him.

"About time you had money of your own. Doesn't mean you have to spend all of it, but you need some in your pocket or purses."

Stella blinked as if she might cry. "Papa, this is your bonus. You worked so hard. I can't take your money when you provide for us."

He shook his head. "No, you three and your sweet mother are why I work. Go, now. Have a nice walk there and back."

He nodded at Finn and turned back to his chair by the stove.

Finn took Stella's elbow to guide her down the steps. "Come, let's get to the Spencer store before the droves o' others sure to be on their way."

Finn's three companions appeared lighthearted as they strolled toward the next town. Fall was upon them and even this far south a few of the trees had turned gold. A light breeze kept the sun's rays from overheating them.

Behind and in front of them other people from Lignite made their way toward Spencer.

"Isn't this a lovely day? Look at all the wildflowers." Stella asked.

"I've learned the names o' a few. The woman who raised me brother in law is a healer who knows the names o' them all and she's taught me ma and sister a bit."

"I recognize yellow evening primrose and yellow broomweed and sunflowers. Oh, and the white flowers are milkweed. I'm not sure of the others."

He gestured to where a vine covered a fence. "That's orange trumpet flower. The vine along the road with pink flowers is wild morning glory."

Lance skipped a stone at tree. "Mama sent a long list. I hope she sent enough scrip. If we went over at the store in Lignite, Mr. Frampton put it on our tab."

Nellie hugged his shoulders. "Don't worry. Mama knows the cost of everything, so I'm sure you'll have enough."

Finn said, "Aye, and I've my bit along if you run short. As often as I've eaten with you, 'tis only right I contribute."

When they reached Spencer, the store was crowded. Stella and Nettie wanted to see everything. Lance did, too. Finn was content to let the Claytons look their fill.

At the cash register, a sign proclaimed
"Scrip worth 75 cents on the dollar."

Finn stared at the hand-lettered sign and met the gaze of the owner.

Mr. George scowled. "I've already had my ear chewed off about the sign, but that's what Farland is willing to pay me for the scrip I collect."

Finn nodded. "Sounds like the man. Frankly, I'm surprised it's not less."

The store owner lowered his voice. "Since you mentioned him, O'Neill, I'll confess he only wanted to pay 60 cents. I had to talk him up to 75 cents."

"Sure and 'twas good o' you. Folks must have food and he gouges somethin' awful on his prices. Naturally he wouldn't want folks to know how much."

"I hope you'll spread the word I'm not to blame." He turned to add up someone's purchases.

Finn browsed the store. When he reached the Clayton sisters, Stella beamed at him.

"I can't decide what to buy and neither can Nettie."

He laughed, hoping he didn't offend her. "Sure and you aren't obligated to spend your money. Your father only wanted you to have the option."

"We won't spend it all. But I must have something to mark today."

Lance carried a book. "I found *Huckleberry Finn* for a quarter so I'll have 75 cents left for another day. Isn't it funny his last name is the same as your first?"

"Sure and I vow you'll like that book."

"You've read it?"

"Aye, that I have. Me brother in law and his family have more books than I knew existed before I met them. Say, if you've finished the other one, would you mind loaning it to Mick Gallagher, the lad in the hospital?"

Lance laughed. "Mama already took it to him. She even read to him for a while. She said he's a nice man."

"His family all died back in Ireland, so he's all alone in the world.

80

Being shut up is making him that depressed."

His face turned thoughtful. "I guess I could visit him."

Finn laid a hand on the boy's shoulder. "You'll be doing him a good turn if you do. Can't imagine being stuck in bed for three months, can you?"

Mr. George called to him. "O'Neill, I've something that might interest you."

Finn weaved through the crowd to the counter.

Mr. George reached for a case, opened it and took out a violin and bow. "Just got this yesterday and thought of you. I'll make you a good deal."

"May I see how it plays?"

When the storekeeper handed it over, Finn plucked the strings, tuned the instrument, and tightened the bow strings. Then he placed the chin rest under his jaw, and struck up a tune. Several customers gathered round to listen.

The tune sounded clear and sweet. He wanted this violin more than he could let Mr. George know. "Sounds good enough for a used fiddle. And how much are you asking?"

Mr. George crossed his arms. "Five dollars. You can see it's in good condition and has the case plus you're the first to see it."

Finn pretended to mull over the price. He'd give twice that for this instrument. "Well, if you'll be taking scrip, then we've a deal."

"Done. How's the concertina working out?" Mr. George counted Finn's scrip and rang up the sale.

"Good, but the fiddle is me first choice."

Mr. George chuckled. "Wish I'd known that before I named the price."

Finn smiled at the store owner. "But 'tis glad I am you didn't."

A strident voice spoke behind him. "Well, I'm not surprised to find you here."

When Finn turned, James Llewellyn stood in front of him. "Hello, James. I suppose most people will come today since Farland announced our scrip is good here."

James stared at the fiddle. "You bought another instrument. What are you doing, planning a band?"

Puzzled at James's aggressive stance, Finn said, "Sure and that would be a fine idea. Will you be joinin' us?"

"Most Welsh are musical but not me." He stared at the store's back. "I suppose Stella Clayton walked here with you."

"All three Claytons did. Will you join us going back?"

James appeared surprised at the offer. "Maybe I will at that if your invitation is real."

"Sure and you're welcome. Now, I might buy meself a sarsaparilla. What are you here for or are you just looking around?"

James's posture relaxed. "Thought I might get me a new shirt."

"Aye, George has some nice ones. I was thinkin' the same, but I spent me scrip on this fiddle."

James spotted the sign. "What's this? He's trying to cheat us."

Finn edged in front of James. "No, 'tis all Farland will pay for the scrip. You'll still save over what you'd spend in Lignite."

James picked up a red shirt. Finn could see the man's lips move as he converted the price. "I see what you mean." He took the shirt to the counter and paid.

Stella carried a handkerchief. "This is a dime, but isn't it lovely?"

Nettie, who walked behind her, carried two similar handkerchiefs. "I want one, too. We're going to each pay a nickel and get one for Mama."

Finn sent Stella a warning look. "James is here and I invited him to walk back with us."

Her eyes widened but she showed no other surprise. "How nice. Hello, Mr. Llewellyn."

Behind Finn, James said, "Ladies. Lance."

Finn asked, "Lance, did you give Mr. George your mother's list?"

"He has it ready in the basket. I paid for my book and he put it in the basket, too."

James leaned his head back. "You bought a book? What's got into you? You could have a knife or a slingshot."

Lance blinked. "I want the book. I read *Tom Sawyer* and I think this takes up where the other left off."

James shook his head. "Thought only girls read books."

Stella and Nettie were each about to protest, but Finn jumped in. "Lots o' men like to read. I read all I can, but then you've seen me, James."

He gave a derisive snort. "Seems a waste of time."

"We all have our likes and dislikes. Well, if we're about ready I'll treat us all to a sarsaparilla and a piece of candy."

Stella smiled at him and her blue-green eyes twinkled. "Really? Oh, I want a piece of chocolate."

Nettie chose red licorice and so did Lance. James said he didn't care for candy. Finn suspected the man was embarrassed to take gifts from him. He paid for the candy then asked George for five drinks. Finn handed over his quarter before he passed the sarsaparillas to his friends.

He popped a piece of chocolate into his mouth and picked up his drink. He carried the fiddle case under his arm. "Shall we head to the butcher's?"

Stella looked around. "Wait. We didn't get anything for Papa."

Lance said, "I did." He held up a harmonica.

"Perfect. Remember he used to have one and we lost it in our move?"

"Okay, then we're set. Careful o' me fiddle when we go through the door."

James rushed to hold the door. "Ladies."

Stella and Nettie glided through. When Finn was about to step outside, James let it close, very narrowly missing his fiddle case. If not for Lance struggling with the large basket, the case might have been damaged. 'Twas good he had the case.

Finn thought James had let the door close deliberately, but he said nothing. They reached the butcher's and Finn went inside. He asked for a beef roast.

The butcher picked up a large one. "I suppose you know Farland is only allowing 60% value for scrip. I know George bargained him up, but I couldn't."

"I'll take that roast and a side of bacon." He paid with the last of his cash. While the owner wrapped his purchases, he thought he might have been foolish spending so much instead of saving for his ranch. No, he'd eaten with the Claytons often enough and hoped to again that he needed to contribute.

When they were on the road, he told Lance, "Why don't we trade? I'll tote that basket if you'll carry me fiddle."

"Naw, I can carry this." Lance walked stooped and appeared to strain under the weight.

The sisters rushed to take some items from Lance's basket and place them in theirs.

Stella apologized, "We're sorry. We were so excited that we forgot why we came."

Nettie held her candy in the arm over which her basket looped and her drink in the other. "Sister, you're smarter to have chosen something sweet that didn't tie up your hands."

On their way again, Finn let Lance carry the basket. The boy needed to feel he did his part. Now that his sisters had helped, he didn't appear to strain under the weight. Stella nudged Nettie and she walked beside James while Stella dropped back with Finn. Lance walked between the two couples.

Finn watched James. The man's jealousy ran deep in spite of anything he said. Why else would he act so against a friend?

Stella took Finn's arm and he forgot about James's pettiness. He was walking with a beautiful woman on a pleasant Fall day. When she smiled up at him, he felt he could do anything.

Yet, he reminded himself, he hadn't found the villain who intended harm to the miners for some unknown reason.

Chapter Eleven

Back at the Clayton home, they unloaded their purchases.

Mrs. Clayton held up her gift. "I've never owned such a fancy handkerchief. This lace edging is lovely."

When Lance handed his father the harmonica, Council laughed. "I declare. You remember when I had one of these?"

"I do, Papa. Can you still play for us?"

James carried a couple of chairs into the living room as if he were at home. They all sat, but Finn chose the bench again and Stella sat beside him. James scowled, then apparently caught himself and his expression changed to a more pleasant one.

Council tested the harmonica then broke into "Camptown Races".

Mrs. Clayton surprised Finn when she picked up the mandolin and strummed the instrument as if she did so daily.

Finn followed along on his new violin that he thought of as a fiddle.

The sisters clapped their hands in time and sang. Looking as if he felt foolish, James clapped along with them.

Council looked at Finn. "I'll bet you know this one." He broke into "Dawning of the Day."

The women sang in English.

Finn waited until they'd reached the end and then he sang the song in Gaelic while the senior Clayton's accompanied him.

Stella clasped her hands at her breast. "That was beautiful. Somehow the lyrics sound more romantic in Irish."

James leaned forward and rested his elbows on his knees. "Liked it better when I could understand the words."

Finn put his violin in the case. "Tomorrow is a work day and one I won't enjoy near as much as the past few weeks."

James stared at him. "Why not?"

Finn stood. "I've been transferred to Johann Swensen's crew because o' the fire. Farland says I'm too comfortable...no, he said 'cozy' on Clayton's crew."

James stood also. "Swensen's. Whew, tough, man. No more bonuses for you."

"So I've heard." Finn shook Council's hand. "Sure and 'twas great working with you and your crew."

He turned to Mrs. Clayton. "Thank you for the meal and the music."

He bowed. "Ladies, Lance, 'twas a pleasure."

When he left, James surprised him by coming along.

"What did Farland say to you?"

"Chewed me out for the fire even though he didn't accuse me o' being a part o' the blaze. Then he told me I was 'too cozy' with Clayton's crew and transferred me to Swensen's starting in the morning."

"Man, that's rough. Swensen's always at the bottom of the board. Don't know why. Maybe he lets his sons loaf on the job."

"Guess I'll find out tomorrow morning."

Once they were back in the bunkhouse, Finn stopped to let Aleski know what had happened.

"Well, I'll be damned if that don't beat everything. Guess we won't be winning the bonus this month."

Jose was listening. "I'm sorry for you, but I have wonderful news. One of the families is moving out this week and I can send for my Maria."

Finn shook the man's hand. "Hey, that's great. When will she arrive?"

"I sent a wire today. But she no send one back yet. Maybe she will just come here."

"Congratulations. Now all we need is for Aleski's wife to show up."

Looking solemn, Aleski shook his head. "I don't have enough saved yet. I need more bonuses."

"Sorry, a man needs his wife and child with him." Finn felt guilty for spending his cash on himself and the concertina.

"Good of you to say, Finn. None of us has cash, that's the problem. I'm going to try to exchange scrip for cash with Farland. If I take fifty cents on the dollar, maybe he'll trade."

Finn lowered his voice. "Don't offer him that. Ask for seventy-five cents on the dollar and let him talk you down. He's a greedy man." He related what Mr. George had said.

"Thanks, Finn. I'll do that. The worst that can happen is he says no."

The next morning, Finn reported to Johann Swensen. He was introduced to Swensen's three sons, Hans, Joe, and Peter, as well as Ralph Evans and his son, Junior.

Swensen said, "Toby, another of Ralph's sons, was sent to Clayton's crew in your place. Now let's get busy."

They traveled down the shaky elevator and then into a separate tunnel from the one where Clayton worked. Right away, Junior bumped into Finn, knocking him against the tunnel wall. He might have thought it was accidental, but he spotted the smile Junior exchanged with his father.

After a few more feet, Hans bumped into Finn, almost sending him to his knees.

Finn was stuck in hell with five devils. He stood with his back toward the tunnel wall, his feet braced, and faced the men. "All right. This had better stop right now. No wonder this crew is at the bottom of the board. Stay out o' me way and let me work. Wouldn't hurt you to do the same."

Johann glared at him. "What are you squawking about?"

"As if you didn't see Junior and Hans knock into me. I'm telling you, I don't have time for games. I came here to work."

Ralph Sr. said, "Watch yourself, O'Neill, or you could get injured."

Ignoring the others, Finn set to working the coal and left them standing to stare at him. In a few minutes, they started working too. But they were either clumsy or lazy or both. He out-produced any two of them. Three if you counted Peter, the youngest of the lot.

Not hard to see where the boys got their mean streaks. No doubt their fathers had talked jealously about Council Clayton. Had they started the rumors or just fed them?

Peter and Joe looked about the same age as Lance and clearly didn't want to be here. Easy to understand why they resented Lance being able to stay at home.

All morning he worked as fast as he could. By noon, his output far exceeded any two of the others.

Over lunch, Swensen asked, "Where'd you learn to work so fast?"

"From watching Council Clayton. He can mine more coal than anyone I've ever seen."

Ralph Sr. said, "What's the point. Pay's the same no matter how hard you work."

Swensen stared at his friend. "Wouldn't it be nice to win a bonus? Or just not be the bottom of the board?"

Junior shrugged. "Don't seem to matter. Bonus ain't much anyway. Why kill ourselves?"

"Back to work." Swensen stomped off.

Junior glared at Finn. "See what you started. I ought to toss you down the pit."

Swensen yelled, "Junior, get over here. That goes for all of you. Anything happens to O'Neill, I'll know who to blame."

Finn kept to himself and worked at his steady rate for the rest of the day. When the day was over, he could hardly wait to get up on top of the ground. He walked toward the bunkhouse without a word to his coworkers.

He washed up, wishing he could wash away the entire day.

Aleski appeared beside him. "How did the day go?"

Finn dried his face and hands. "I'm surprised I'm alive. Those are the laziest, most worthless men I've had the misfortune to meet."

"Suspected as much. The Evans kid who came on our crew don't know his ass from a hole in the ground. If his dad weren't a miner, he'd be fired. We can kiss a bonus goodbye."

He shook his head. "Well, it won't be Swensen's crew who wins. I've already been threatened by Ralph Evans Jr. for working too hard. Says I set a bad example."

"Say, maybe you should see Adams and ask to be moved to another crew. I don't like any of the Swensen or Evans families."

"Naw, Adams couldn't contradict Farland's orders. Afraid I'm stuck."

"Right. If you need some help…um, reasoning with that crew, let me know. My friends and I will 'speak' to them convincingly."

"Thanks, Aleski. I appreciate the thought."

Even though he wouldn't ask for Aleski's help, the man's offer and support meant a lot. They went in to dinner.

James sat beside Finn. "How'd it go with the new crew?"

Finn sent him a glower.

"That bad?"

"Worse than you can imagine." He repeated what he'd told Aleski.

"Man, that crew sounds lazy. No wonder they've never won a bonus."

Finn leaned in to ask, "Is it true that they're in no danger o' being fired?"

James shrugged. "I don't know. Appears there's a shortage of miners. And with the fire, men are leaving."

Finn was shocked. "Already?"

James sopped gravy with his bread. "Yeah, quite a bit of turnover anyway since the accidents started."

"I didn't realize that. Who do you think's behind the trouble?"

James looked at his plate, spearing a stray piece of potato. "I can't say. Hartford wants a union, but he's not the only one. Besides, I don't think he'd cause trouble other than talk."

"I agree. He's that sure a union would help miners, but he doesn't appear the sort to conspire to kill men."

"As you learned today, everyone is willing to kill for something." James picked up his plate and headed for the door.

Finn sat thinking and listening to the buzz of voices around him. Finally, he stood and carried his plate to the dish bin. He stepped outside for a few minutes' walk, but fatigue dragged at him. Or, mayhap 'twas disgust.

He went in, shucked off his clothes, and lay on his bunk. What was he to do about his new crew? He'd gone from working with men he admired to working with the dregs of humanity. Damned if he'd let them defeat him.

James came in from outside and plopped on his bunk. "Bet you're tired tonight."

"Disgusted. I worked hard on Clayton's crew, but the men were all hard workers and friendly. There was respect between us and for Clayton."

James chuckled. "Toby Evans must be a shock to them."

"Huh, I imagine he's the one who had the shock. Clayton would expect him to do his share. He's probably exhausted after actually working for the first time in his life."

James turned on his side facing away from Finn. "Good luck tomorrow."

"Thanks, you too." Finn lay looking at the moonlight from the window create patterns on the ceiling.

Laughter came from the card players. He hoped Aleski was winning again and that Farland would trade scrip for cash but he wondered at the Polish man's stamina. Aleski must need only a few hours' sleep.

Finn resolved to go ask Stella for a walk tomorrow after work. He refused to let Swensen's crew change his routine. They could try intimidating him all they wanted, but he wasn't scaring off.

Yeah, he admitted he'd been scared today. Being in a tunnel so far underground with no one to help him if he was attacked had caught him off guard. There were other crews nearby, but he had no idea if they would stop work to investigate a fight. Tomorrow, he was going in ready.

The next morning, he nodded and said, "Good morning." After that he rode the elevator without a word to the others.

While they lit their hat candles, Ralph Evans said, "That Clayton jumped all over Toby. He has his nerve talking to my boy like he did. And none of the others defended Toby neither."

"What'd you expect? You taught him to do only as much as he could get by with. Clayton expects a fair day's work for a day's pay. Did you think everyone went through life giving the minimum?" Finn strode down the tunnel to where he'd stopped the previous day.

Ralph caught up to him. "You think you're better 'n we are, don'tcha?"

Finn met the man's stare. "I'm no better than any other man, but I'm every damn bit as good."

Swensen said, "Get to work and quit bitchin'."

Finn set to work, appearing to ignore the others but not trusting them enough to do so. He especially kept his eye on Junior. The man already had a paunch developing and he couldn't be much over twenty years old. And he'd tried once to make Finn fall, so there was no giving him a second opportunity.

At noon, Finn ate at the edge of the others.

Junior came over beside him. "Guess I scared you yesterday. I could throw you into the pit under the elevator anytime I want, you know."

"Oh? You the one killing others around here?"

Junior's brow furrowed. "What do you mean? I never killed nobody."

"Then don't threaten me. Someone has caused trouble and several men died. Mick Gallagher almost died and is in the hospital now."

Junior forked a thumb at his own chest. "Don't blame me. I don't know Gallagher. You're the one I don't like."

Finn got in his face. "That makes us even, for I don't like you either. You're a lazy bully and I've got no time for your kind. I'm here to do a job and that's mine coal. What the hell are you here for?"

"I'm a miner too. Just because you think you're too good for us, don't think you are."

Swensen slapped Junior upside the head. "I said quit your bitchin'. Time to go back to work." He pointed at Junior. "And I mean work."

Grumbling, the two Evans men went to the seam of coal and started picking it loose. Finn still outworked both of them combined.

All three of the Swensen boys worked harder, but Joe and Peter were young. Neither could do the work of a man. Finn wondered how much pay they received. Even though they'd bullied and ganged up on Lance, he sympathized with the lads.

He hated this life now, but he'd have hated it more at their age. At least he had hope of leaving, whether to his ranch or back to Dallas's. The Swensen boys could only look forward to a dreary life underground.

At the end of the day, Swensen stopped Finn. "I may have misjudged you, O'Neill. You're a hard worker. We might get off the bottom of the board this month."

Surprised, he forced a smile. "I hope so. Sure and 'tis someone else's turn to be last."

He walked back to the wash up area a little less fatigued than the previous day. Darned if he wouldn't go see Stella. Watching her pretty face light up would improve his disposition a hundred percent.

He cleaned up and ate quickly before striding toward her home. When he rapped on the door, they were just finishing supper and invited him in.

"I came to ask Miss Stella to walk with me."

Council smiled. "We enjoyed the roast. You're spoiling us."

Mrs. Clayton rushed to hug him. "That's the first beef roast we've had in ever so long. I hated to serve it without you, but we were afraid of it spoiling unless we cooked it."

"I'm that glad you enjoyed the meat. 'Tis often enough you've fed me that I owe you a bit o' food in payment."

"Oh, you're always welcome, Mr. O'Neill." Her sweet face convinced him she meant her words.

Stella threw her shawl around her. Today she wore a blue dress that made her eyes look more blue than green. True the garment had seen a bit of wear, but she looked lovely. He wondered if she'd knitted the cream shawl she wore.

He offered his arm and they went on their way.

"How has your new crew been?"

"Ach, don't ask. 'Tis even worse than I feared. I thought yesterday Junior Evans would kill me. Today Swensen told him to lay off, but not in those words. I can't repeat to a lady what Swensen said."

Alarm spread across her perfect face. "My goodness, Finn. I hope you aren't in danger. Mining is hazardous enough without your crew mates acting violent."

"Sure and 'tis straightened out they are. Junior is still apt to attack me, but he's that slow and not so strong as me."

She appeared unsatisfied with his answer. "If he hits you from behind, he doesn't have to be stronger than you. Oh, Finn, go back to Mr. Farland and ask him to change you out of that crew."

"I can't, Stella. I'll be fine, don't you worry your beautiful head." He patted her hand where it rested on his arm.

Sparks ignited in her eyes and he sensed her body tense. "Hearing things like that makes me so mad. Do you think I'm stupid that you can pat me and tell me not to worry?"

"Just the opposite. You're the smartest woman I've ever known. Maybe the smartest person, although Dallas's aunt Kathryn is smart as a whip. 'Tis thinking I am that you'll like her. And I know she'll think a lot o' you."

She sighed. "When I think I'm mad at you, you say something irresistible."

"Ah, then I hope 'tis always so. You're fierce when you're angry and I don't want to be on the receivin' end o' your temper." He laughed and did a fast dance step and twirled her around before replacing her hand on his arm.

"Don't start about my temper or you'll rile me." Her eyes sparkled with mirth belying her words. "You're very talented musically. Seems a shame you're underground all day."

"To me, too. I've no fondness for the mine. I'll be that glad when I can quit." He caught himself too late. He'd been so careful to watch his tongue, but being with Stella relaxed him and his thoughts had slipped out before his mind caught them.

Surprise showing on her face, she peered at him. "What do you mean? Are you quitting soon?"

He shook his head. "Just meant that I want to have me ranch. Ranching's a good life, Stella. Hard, but there are slack times when a body can relax in front o' the fire. Best of all, ranching happens entirely above ground."

She laughed. "You're a dreamer, Finn O'Neill, but I like hearing your dreams."

"Mine will come true. You wait and you'll see I speak true."

Chapter Twelve

Finn rubbed sleep from his eyes before he took his turn cranking the elevator platform to the level where Swensen's crew worked with three other crews. They stepped from the shaky conveyance and trudged to where they'd left off the previous workday.

He set to work immediately. Another day in the underworld. Finn thought of the stories Dallas had told of the Greek myths and could understand why Hades needed Persephone to brighten his life. That thought led him to consider Stella and the way his time with her lightened the weight of this job.

Realizing she believed him only a dreamer instead of a potential rancher made him value her friendship more. Was theirs only friendship? His attraction to her increased as he knew her better, not the other way around as he'd hoped.

At lunch, Ralph Senior stood behind him while Junior pushed into him and he tripped over Senior's extended leg.

Fury blinded him and he leapt to his feet, slinging muddy water from his clothes and ready to end lunch with a brawl.

Swensen's arm at his chest stopped him. "There'll be no more of that. Ralph, you and Junior are on report to Adams. Once more and Adams will fire you."

The crew chief stepped in front of Senior. "You're a grown man. What kind of example are you setting for your kids?"

Ralph screwed his face in derision. "They know where their food comes from. Why are you takin' up for this interloper who thinks he's better 'n us?"

Swensen poked Ralph Senior in the chest. "Matters not to me whether you like O'Neill or not, you'll get along and act your age. Quit worrying about him and do your job."

Junior spoke low. "I ain't forgettin' you caused us to get a bad mark."

Finn only shook his head. How could a troublemaker be stupid enough to blame someone else for his actions? The father and son reminded him of Tom Williams, the man who'd targeted his family before they'd met Dallas earlier in the year.

He glared at the younger Evans. "You heard Swensen. Act your age and get to work."

Junior grumbled under his breath as he walked away.

Finn knew he hadn't seen the last of this. The Evans men were bullies who hated anyone who outshone them in any way. With their low standards, that meant everyone. What a way to go through life.

After they left the mine that evening, Junior grabbed Finn's shoulder. As Finn turned, Junior slugged him. Finn hit the ground with a wham that knocked the air from his lungs.

Men gathered around as Finn rose. He rubbed his jaw, which hurt like a sledgehammer had hit him. "Can't give a man warning, is that right, Junior?"

The other man lunged at him. Finn sidestepped and chopped across the base of Junior's neck. He would have followed through but Senior shoved him from behind.

Shouts arose from the other men about foul play and cheating. Two men grabbed Senior and held him back. Finn rose again but the delay had given Junior time to stand. He shook his head as if to clear either his mind or vision.

"Come at me fair, man, or do you need your papa to help you?" Finn beckoned to Junior.

With a growl, Junior rushed at him.

After growing up with a band of Irish Travelers, Finn knew how to fight even though he avoided conflict. He supposed mining camps provided similar training. Perhaps being a bully meant Junior didn't have to fight his battles alone, for he hadn't made a good choice.

Finn stepped aside again and repeated his earlier chop. Junior dropped to his knees but grabbed Finn's ankle. Finn twisted as he fell and kicked Junior in the face. The sound of the man's nose crunching accompanied his own crash to the ground.

He jumped to his feet quickly and braced for the next assault. His opponent staggered up with blood gushing from his nose. Junior spit out a tooth and came toward Finn.

Ben Adams yelled, "Stop this right now."

Finn stepped back but Junior acted as if he hadn't heard the order.

Sheriff Thad Quinton wielded a billy club. "Stop there or you'll feel this on your skull."

The two men holding back Ralph Senior released him.

Senior grabbed his son's arm. "Come on, Junior, the sheriff said to stop."

Junior stared at his father as if dazed but stopped his aggressive advance.

The lawman stared from Finn to Junior. "What's the meaning of this? I won't have brawling in my town."

Junior said, "He started it."

Numerous voices yelled liar and cheat.

Swensen stepped up. "I had to threaten the two Evans men in the shaft today. They wouldn't stop mischief directed at O'Neill. Told Ralph Senior and Junior I was turning in their name to Adams here. They couldn't let it go and attacked O'Neill as soon as we were off work."

Adams looked at the two Evans men. "You're both fired. You can pick up your pay tomorrow and have one week to move out."

Ralph Senior stared at the foreman. "You can't do that. I've got a family to feed."

Adams pointed at him. "You should have thought of that before you caused trouble."

The sheriff waved his billy club. "Okay, men, nothing else to see here. Get on your way." He pointed the club at Finn. "I'll be watching and there better not be any more trouble involving you."

Finn held up his hands and walked away.

Council kept in step beside him. "You okay?"

"Yeah, other than my jaw feels like a mule kicked it."

"Make that a jackass and you'd be right. Well, I'll go on home. You better hit the hay and give your head some extra rest."

"I expect that's true. Probably feel like a giant pumpkin by morning."

Council chuckled. "Save some for pie."

On his other side, Aleski and Jose had joined him.

Aleski said, "We have big news. Farland exchanged me fifty cents on the dollar like you said. I sent for my wife and son. I don't know how long the journey will take, but I'm happy they will finally be here with me.'

"Say, that's great news. How about you, Jose?"

The man was more animated than Finn had ever seen him. "Maria, she wire she will be here in on Friday."

"Wonderful. Wish we could celebrate. Maybe on Saturday night."

"Sí, we will have a fiesta." Jose danced ahead a few steps.

***

Friday morning, Swensen's crew was the first in rotation to use the elevator platform. They climbed on and Finn braced himself for the worst part of his morning, his trip on what seemed a rickety, swaying descent. Ascending in the evening was as bad, but then he had leaving the mine for the day to comfort him.

He'd spoken to Clayton and his former crew mates as he passed them. Aleski was back at the longhouse with a bad stomach ache, but the rest of the crew would be the next group to follow. Swensen's crew climbed aboard and Finn and Junior turned the crank that lowered them to their tunnel.

As he watched the cable unroll as they descended deeper into the mine, Finn was startled by the sight of broken threads in the wire rope.

"Quick, Hans, reverse and take us to the top as fast as you can."

"What?" The younger man stared at him.

"What are you talking about?" The elder Swensen demanded.

Clutching the handle, Finn nodded at the spot above his head. "Look at the cable."

Another of the threads pulled free, leaving less than half the cable supporting the platform.

Swenson yelled, "Take us up fast."

Finn and Hans reeled the line back around the carrier frantic to reach above the damaged section. When they were well above where the cable would be secure, they slowed but kept turning the handles. Not until they were safely able to step off the platform did Finn relax.

Ben Adams scowled at them. "You men decide not to work today?"

Swensen glared at the foreman. "You're supposed to check the cable. We like to have fell to our death."

"That's a new cable and only been on there two days. I watched it reeled on. There's nothing wrong with the cable."

Swensen gestured to the platform. "Yeah? Then why is over half the wire broken through about fifty feet down?"

Adams scowl changed to a shocked expression. "What?" He rushed to the cable. "Men, help me unroll this cable."

Finn and Hans swung the platform sideways to get it over firm ground before unwinding the cable to reach the damaged portion. When they had enough line, they tugged the cable toward the foreman for inspection.

Anger turned his face dark red. "This isn't broken, the wire strands have been deliberately cut. No one is using this until the cable has been replaced."

Council asked, "Should we use the night crews' platform or the one for the coal cars?"

Adams shook his head. "No one is using anything until I've checked into this. I'm pretty damned tired of these incidents. I find out who's responsible and he's a dead man."

Swensen asked, "So, we go home and lose a day's pay?"

The foreman glared at him. "You rather lose your life? Go home. I'll have to inform Mr. Farland about this latest sabotage."

Finn walked with Council Clayton and his crew. "Surprised Adams closed the mine for today?"

Council glanced over his shoulder. "First time I've known that to happen. Would have thought our lives were disposable as long as production stayed on schedule. Probably would have been if Farland were consulted before Adams acted."

"I can't decide if this was directed at you or at me."

Council met his gaze. "Wondered the same thing. Schedule for using the elevator is easy to figure out. If your crew safely unloaded, mine would have been sure to fall."

"Who has time and means to cut the cable?"

Council shook his head. "Anyone could have during the night. The night crew's working on another section this week and using the other elevator."

Obviously overhearing them, Jose said, "I was up late watching the card players but heard nothing."

Finn wondered. "You weren't listening for something like this. A man slipping out for the privy would go unnoticed. But the culprit might not be single."

Jose appeared thoughtful. "You're right on both counts. I wouldn't pay attention to a man slipping out because I'd think he was going to the outhouse nor would I give any notice to how long he was gone. As you say, the man responsible might be married and not from our longhouse."

Finn had another chewing out to look forward to, for he expected to be called before Farland and either fired or threatened. One thing, he'd eliminated Swensen as the one responsible, for the man wouldn't risk himself and two of his sons. That left him just lazy and ineffective as a crew leader.

When they reached the place where the single men and married separated, Finn paused. "Sir, I'd like to meet Stella today at her school? I've not seen the inside."

"She'll probably enjoy showing it off. I don't know what to do with an extra day off."

"Take Mrs. Clayton somewhere. Maybe even just a picnic."

"Sounds good. I'll let her choose."

Aleski strolled up. "Bosko and Pakulski are going with me to look at the work on the store. Want to come?"

"May as well. Place ought to be about finished by now." Finn knew the other two men by sight as the card players with Aleski each night. Kasper Bosko and Piotr Pakulski had known Aleski at home and were distant relatives.

Bosko said, "The men throw it up fast. Don't think it's well built, but then what is here?"

They reached the structure. Charred wood had been carted off and new wood joined the undamaged section. The outside appeared complete and painters brushed on gray paint.

Finn crossed his arms. "Surprised they're painting the building. Might as well start with gray since that's the color everything eventually becomes."

Aleski stood with hands in his pocket. "I heard Farland's new stock has partially arrived, but the interior isn't quite finished out yet. By the end of the week, we'll be back spending our scrip here."

Finn thought the store's fresh paint at least added a bright spot where most mine buildings were left unpainted. "Shame we can't continue to shop in Spencer. I like that town much better."

Aleski rubbed his hands together. "Anyone for a game of cards?"

All three of the others groaned.

Finn laughed and clapped Aleski on the shoulder. "I'll see you later."

He walked to the Clayton home. Lance answered his knock.

"I'm going to Spencer. Ask your mom if she needs anything."

Lance held open the door. "Sure. Can I come?"

"Why not?" Finn stood on the porch taking in the bright October sunshine. The bright blue sky overhead held not a cloud. He would be filled with cheer at a free day if not for the fact that someone had tried to kill him. That tended to ruin an otherwise good day.

Chapter Thirteen

Finn collected his mail. He stuffed the note from Farland into his pocket but tore open the one from Cenora.

Dear Finn,

You must have wondered if you're an uncle yet. On October 1st your nephew Houston Brendan McClintock was born. He weighed 8 and a half pounds so I suppose he will be tall like his da. He's a good baby. Dallas is that proud he struts like one of the roosters.

Vourneen is doing well and will have her baby about Christmas. She and Mac still live in the caravan, but Mac has a <u>real</u> job. Sort of. He's working with Vourneen's father and learning to repair watches and guns and mend metal pots and pans. Mac plans to add to his small salary from Mr. McDonald by painting buildings so he and Vourneen can rent a house soon. (Mac promises he'll use good paint and do a fine job. I believe he will this time.)

Ma and Da are fine and appear happier than I ever remember them. Da has giant pumpkins in his garden and plans to enter them in the fair this month. He's selling plenty of produce and milk and eggs and feeling proud of the money he's saved.

We are so happy, and wish you were here to share with us. I hope you finish there soon. We miss you.

Love,

Your sister Cenora

He waved the letter overhead. "How about this…I'm an uncle. Hey, everyone, I'm an uncle. Me sister had a boy. Parents and babe are doing fine."

Amid congratulations and laughter, he reread Cenora's words. How he wished he were home with his family. The thought staggered him. For years he'd looked forward to leaving family behind and roaming on his own. Now, all he wanted was to be in McClintock Falls near his family. He'd never held a baby but he yearned to hold Houston Brendan McClintock.

He strolled through the store until he reached the children's clothes. A woman with a cheerful countenance and who appeared vaguely familiar stood there. She had dark brown hair and wore a tan wrap.

"Ma'am, what would a newborn babe need? That is, something I could mail or ship?"

She tilted her head and appeared to consider his request. "A blanket would be nice since winter's coming. A toy that might last. Clothing is nice, but they grow so fast I'm sure your sister already has things for the lad to wear. A cup or spoon for later would be useful."

"Thank you. I've no experience with babies you see, so I need guidance."

She held up a blue blanket and a small cup and spoon. "If you'll be mailing your gift, consider ease of packing. These are light and any would be useful."

"Thank you, ma'am. I'll take all of them."

"I'm Marta Gretsky. You worked with my man until lately."

"Mrs. Gretsky, 'tis an honor. Sure and I thought I should know your name. Your man is a good one and a hard worker."

Her smile broadened and her brown eyes sparkled. "That he is. I hope your sister enjoys your gift."

At the counter, Finn asked the owner. "Have you something to use for mailing these to me sister."

"I heard your announcement, O'Neill, and I've heard you defending me to those who thought I cheated them on the scrip exchange. You give me her address and I'll pack and mail them and won't charge extra for the packing. Been a pleasure doing business with you." The store owner passed a scrap of wrapping paper to Finn with the amount owed for postage.

"Thank you kindly, Mr. George." Finn wrote out Cenora and Dallas's address on the paper and handed over the scrip required.

He turned to Lance. "And have you given Mr. George your mother's list?"

"Yes. Can I look around a bit? I still have two bits of my money."

"Take all the time you need. I've naught to do until your sister's school is done for the day. I'll get us something to gnaw on when we start back."

Finn's mood ran high. An uncle and soon an uncle again. Sure and he'd be home before Mac's babe arrived.

After thirty minutes looking through the store, Lance had chosen nothing. "I can't find what I want. Mama's birthday is in a week."

"Your sisters bought her a handkerchief. Mayhap she'd like a pair o' gloves for Sunday."

"Yeah? Let me see how much they cost." Lanced headed to the women's area. He sorted through the stack of lady's gloves. "The black pair is twenty cents."

"They look fine. You'll still have a nickel to save for another day."

"I might get a sweet."

Finn held up his package. "I have us each a sarsaparilla, a sticky bun, and a pickled egg. 'Tis a picnic we'll have before we start back to Lignite."

"That's nice of you, Finn. I'll pay for these and the things Mama ordered."

When they were outside, they bypassed the bench where one of the miners rested.

Walking toward Lignite, Finn spotted an inviting place beneath a live oak tree. "Let's eat over there."

Lance looked longingly at the parcel Finn carried. "I sure am hungry and I've never had a pickled egg."

He strode off the road and up to the tree. "Aye, I could eat a bite meself. 'Tis not the tastiest o' meals, but 'twill keep us going 'til supper. On days like this, eating in the open air is a treat." Peering around, he saw nothing to prevent them eating their simple fare in peace.

They sat and he opened the parcel of buns and eggs then passed Lance his share. In companionable silence, they watched those passing on the road.

When they'd finished the simple meal, Finn drained the last of the sarsaparilla from the bottle before bundling up the rubbish. He stood and brushed leaves and twigs from his clothes. Lance rose and did the same. They were headed to the road when a familiar voice hailed them.

James called, "Hey, you two. Eating again?"

"Aye, are you going to Spencer or returning to Lignite?" Finn didn't say home, because that's not how he thought of the mining town.

"Back. Want to join me?"

Finn looked at Lance for confirmation before saying, "Wouldn't that be nice?"

When they reached the road, he asked, "Did you hear that Jose's wife will be here tomorrow? We're planning a party to celebrate, what he calls a fiesta, and everyone's invited."

James nodded. "Yeah? I heard something about that but didn't know everyone was invited. What happens at a fiesta?"

"Far as I know, there'll be food, dancing, and music. Some o' the ladies are taking care o' rounding up the food. Jose lined up other Mexican men who'll play for the dance."

"So you're not supplying the music, huh?"

"Not this time." Finn intended to ask Stella to dance several times. In fact, he hoped he could have her to himself all evening, but he knew that would be impossible.

The three of them arrived in Lignite about two. Finn and James walked toward the longhouse. Several men had rigged a game of bowls on the side of the longhouse. Finn paused to watch, but today the game didn't hold his interest.

Nearby, men played a makeshift game of football. Others yelled and egged the players to defeat one team or the other. He stood at the sidelines until time to head to the school.

As he ambled toward the building converted to a school, children poured out of the structure. He hurried to the door. Sticking his head inside, he spotted her cleaning the blackboard.

Didn't she look a picture? Her blue skirts swayed provocatively with her movements. Her beautiful hair was piled high on her head. He preferred the tresses hanging down her back.

Rapping on the doorjamb, he called to her, "Stella? May I come in?"

She whirled to face him, surprise evident. "Finn? What on earth are you doing off work at this time of day?"

He explained about the mine closing. "I told your father I'd meet you here and ask you to go with me to the restaurant at the hotel."

She wiped her hands on a cloth. "Really? How exciting."

Nettie glided into the room. "I thought I heard your voice, Mr. O'Neill. Has something happened at the mine?"

"You forgot to call me Finn." Repeating the story, he ended with, "I've come to steal your sister for the evening."

Nettie laughed. "Then I'll take myself home. Have a nice time."

When her sister had left, Stella gestured around her. "Here's the school. What do you think?"

Turning slowly, he surveyed the room. "Aye, 'tis much as I imagined. I thought there'd be tables or desks for the students."

"There should be, but Farland won't spend the money." She took his arm and tugged him into the next room.

"This is where Nettie teaches. Many of her students don't speak English, so most of her time is spent teaching a common language. The hope is the students will teach their parents."

"Do they?"

She sighed. "A little, but for the most part the mothers don't bother. The fathers have to learn a little English in order to work."

He enjoyed the tour of the small school. Wouldn't he have loved being a student here? At least, he thought he would. Mayhap he'd have been as eager to leave as the students rushing out a few minutes ago.

In the cloakroom, he pulled her to him for a kiss. "I can't tell you how much I've looked forward to seeing you today. 'Twas on me mind since last I saw you."

Blushing, she laid her hands on his chest. "I've looked forward to seeing you again also."

He tipped her chin so her beautiful blue-green eyes met his gaze. "Will you go with me to the fiesta tomorrow?"

"I'd be pleased to do so. Mama, Nettie, and I are cooking special dishes for the big day. I'm glad Jose and his wife will be apart no longer. The house they've been assigned is only three doors down from ours."

Gently brushing a stray tendril from her face, he thought how lucky he was this lovely and intelligent woman let him kiss her. "Never saw a happier man. Shall we go to supper?"

She beamed up at him as she laid her hand on his arm. "I think if we're going to the restaurant, we're going to dinner."

He laughed. "Aye, 'tis probably true."

They continued up the hill, waving to those who walked on the other side of the road and offering a good evening to others.

"I stayed at the hotel my first night in Lignite. The dining room food is good enough, but your mother's is better."

"I'll tell her you said so. She'll be pleased."

At the restaurant, they were seated near a window. "Not a great view, but at least we can see outside."

Gazing around the dining room, Stella appeared to take in everything. "I've not eaten here. When we came, the hotel hadn't been completed."

"Where did you stay?"

"Our house was ready and we moved in. At least Mr. Farland had furnished the place, although you may have noticed there aren't enough places to sit comfortably."

"Aye, he shorted you on chairs and there's no sofa. 'Tis my opinion the man is that stingy with his workers, I'm surprised he provided anything in the way o' furniture."

"He told us we could order whatever else we wanted through the store. We never have, as you can tell. With five of us, Papa's paycheck doesn't go far. I don't know how those with huge families manage."

"Not well, I imagine. But 'tis important for families to stay together."

"That's what I think. Finn, can you think of something healthier Papa can do to earn a living wage?"

"Not offhand, but 'tis sure and I'll be thinking on the problem." He'd write to Cenora and have her set Dallas thinking on the same.

In his planning for the future, Finn intended Stella and her family to come to McClintock Falls with him. But Council would need a job and so would Nettie. As much as Finn would like to support them as Dallas had done for the O'Neill family, Finn wouldn't have the resources.

He'd not been inside the Lippincott home, but he knew t'was large. Would it be as empty as that of Dallas's when they arrived? Finn didn't care, as long as he could have that ranch.

Cenora had attended teas there on several occasions, so mayhap she could tell him about the rooms. Inwardly, he scolded himself. Unless he discovered Lignite's troublemaker, he wouldn't have his own ranch. He'd have only his single room at Dallas and Cenora's home.

Stella's soft voice interrupted his musing. "You're deep in thought."

"With such a beautiful woman across from me, mayhap I was dumbstuck."

Her laughter came like silver bells tinkling. "What blarney, Finn O'Neill. What were you really thinking?"

His cheeks heated in a flush. "Today I learned o' me sister's babe arriving and 'tis homesick I am. Just now I was thinking o' Dallas's ranch and Ma and Da and me brother and his wife. Family is important."

"And is that where you plan to ranch someday?"

"Almost. 'Tis the ranch next to that o' Dallas that is me dream. Ah, 'tis a wondrous place, Stella. The house is large and there are strong barns and fences. The river runs through so there's water a plenty."

Her voice was sharp when she asked, "And does the owner accept scrip?"

He reeled back as if she'd slapped him. Indeed she might as well, so harsh was her tone and filled with bitterness.

Immediately, a sorrowful expression crossed her face and she reached across the table and clasped his hand. "I'm sorry, Finn, that was mean. I-I hope you get your ranch and it's everything you've dreamed."

After taking a deep breath, he calmed the pain her stabbing comment had caused. Her statement let him know what she truly thought about his dreams. "I know 'tis fanciful I sound."

He tapped the table with his forefinger. "I *will* have me own ranch someday soon. 'Tis all that keeps me going here. I don't like this life even though I've met some fine people. I'll not be sad to leave Lignite."

She withdrew her hand and looked at her plate. "I'll be sorry to lose your friendship."

"And why would you think you'd lose it? A friend is always a friend." How he wished he could speak his heart to her. 'Twas not time so he held back his longing to confess all.

When she raised her head, her gaze was solemn, but she smiled. "That's true." She peered around. "Thank you for bringing me here tonight. This has been a treat."

"For me, too. Will you have more o' anything?"

She shook her head. "The meal was lovely. The bread pudding was good, but I couldn't tell what flavored the sauce."

He chuckled. "Because 'twas brandy. Not something either o' us drinks, I'll wager. But I asked when I stayed here."

They stood and proceeded toward her home. He strolled slowly to extend their time together as long as he could. Ambling casually with her arm on his gave him the thought he could conquer the world. Sure and when she raised her face to gaze at him, he knew he could do anything. Even discover the troublemaker causing all the meanness.

When they arrived at her home, darkness had fallen. Finn stepped onto the porch with her and pulled her into an embrace. He kissed her sweet lips, savoring her surrender.

When she slid her arms around his neck, he deepened the kiss. Her return of his probing tongue proved she had passion. She must care for him or she'd never let him kiss her so fully.

His heart pounded so loud the town must hear. His breathing increased and heat shot through his body. Though he wanted to pull her closer, he didn't want to frighten her with knowing his manhood had reared to life. At the same time, he longed to have her alone and make sweet love to her.

Sounds from inside the house broke them apart. She leaned her head against his chest. Her breathing came in rapid gasps.

His heart's pounding slowed and he caressed her face. "Don't give up on me, sweet Stella. I'll make me dreams come true."

"See that you do, Finn. Don't let your dreams die."

"Don't forget you agreed to go to the fiesta with me tomorrow. I'll be by at half past seven."

"I'll be ready."

Reluctantly, Finn released her and she went inside her home. Running down the steps, he whistled an Irish jig. Sure and life in Lignite had advantages to offset the bad.

The next night, men hurried to clean up after their day's work. Finn changed shirts and britches, slicked back his hair, and shaved again. They had ribbed Jose good-naturedly as he cleared his belongings from the longhouse yesterday.

After making his way to the Clayton home, Finn rapped on the door.

Stella stepped out carrying a plate covered with a towel. She wore her green dress and the ribbon he'd given her tied back her hair.

Finn took the plate. "What am I carrying?"

"An apple cobbler I made. Mama made a pot of stew and Papa is bringing cider and all our metal plates. At these events, everyone brings his own cutlery. We included enough for you."

He glanced over his shoulder. "Your sister and brother coming?"

"Nettie and Lance are already there helping with the decorations."

"Jose is that excited. 'Tis good tomorrow is Sunday so he and Maria have a day to recover from tonight's fiesta."

She waved at Polly and Ulys Young who were just leaving their front porch steps. "How long has it been since Jose came to work here?"

"About six or seven months, I think. Your father would know better than me because 'tis on your father's crew he works."

"Doesn't matter. I just want us to dance at the party and enjoy ourselves."

Her enthusiasm brought a smile to his face. "I've never danced with you. I hope you'll save a lot of dances for me."

"Ah, what if prospective partners swarm around me?" Mischief sparkled in her lovely blue-green eyes.

He refused to let her know how jealous that would make him. "Save me the first and last dance and as many in between as you wish. For myself, I'd like each dance with you. To be polite, though, I'll dance with your mother and sister and Jose's wife." He guided her through the throng of people to set the cobbler on the dessert table.

"You have good manners. Your ma did a good job raising a wild Irish boy."

"She tried. Me sister helped. Both knocked me upside the head enough times 'tis a wonder the marbles in me head don't rattle."

The band struck up a spirited tune and Finn swept Stella onto the dance area. She laughed as he twirled her around, weaving among other dancers. Although only hard packed dirt, no one appeared to mind. He recognized the Mexican tune from his time in McClintock Falls, an area where many Mexican people lived.

As he suspected, many men wanted to dance with Stella. Finn claimed Stella as often as he could. James Llewellyn cut in too many times. The man was deviling him and Stella. Could he not step aside graciously?

At nine, the band broke for supper. His feet were that glad.

"Shall we join the line for supper?" He guided her toward the makeshift tables set up at the side.

She fanned her face. "Good thing this is a cool night or I'd have melted."

"Sure and didn't I tell you'd be the belle of this ball?"

"You cut a swath yourself. I saw you dancing with Mama and Nettie and Polly Young. I wasn't sure who the last woman was."

"Keeping your eye on me, are you? Well, you left out Maria Garza. The last round was with Marta Gretsky. She's a bit shy, but her husband is on your papa's crew."

She leaned close so no one else would overhear. "You'd best take a turn with Ilya Swensen. Her husband isn't dancing much and she looks upset."

He glanced in the direction she indicated. "Aye, 'tis right you are. Were I to have me druthers, I'd dance only with you. We suit well, don't we?"

Her eyes sparkled with mischief. "As dancers, yes, we do."

He wanted to ask about otherwise, but Ralph Evans and Junior pushed through the crowd. A murmur rippled across the crowd as people parted for the angry looking men.

Sheriff Quinton met them before they reached the food. "You no longer work here. This celebration is for the miners employed at Farland Coal Mine and their families."

Senior braced his legs as if ready for a fight. "Two of my sons still work here. My daughter in law is here and brought food." He pointed at

Finn. "You've cost me my livelihood and a place to live. I'll see you pay for the damage."

Wallace Farland broke through the onlookers. "Ralph Evans, you cost yourself your job. I was going to fire you, but your son's fight sped up the process. You would have been fired within a week anyway."

"You've no right to say that. My boys and I never missed a day of work. We been loyal to you and now you're casting us aside."

Farland motioned four security guards forward. "You may have shown up for duty, but you were the lowest producers in the company. Once away from your influence, Jonas turned out to be a good worker. Clayton assures me the same is true of Toby. You've only yourself to blame for losing your job."

The guards escorted the two Evans men away. The confrontation cast a pall over the party. Red-faced Toby and Jonas appeared humiliated.

Council Clayton spoke to the band leader. The men picked up their instruments and broke into a lively tune. Nettie asked Jonas and Mrs. Clayton invited Toby to dance. Appearing reluctant, the young men allowed themselves to be guided into the reel.

When he met her gaze, Stella nodded and set down her plate. As they launched into the dance, other couples followed them. Soon the party mood had returned for most of the attendees. Finn doubted the same was true for the two Evans young men.

He thought it a pity Ralph Evans wasn't the one he'd been hired to catch. But neither Senior nor Junior were smart enough or energetic enough to plan the catastrophes that had plagued the mine. Who had a grudge that deep and was clever enough to follow a devious plan?

Chapter Fourteen

Sunday afternoon, Stella clung to Finn's arm as they hurriedly climbed the hill. "I could hardly concentrate on the Preacher Mitchell's sermon. Was my imagination playing tricks or did he actually go over today?"

"He was that wound up, wasn't he? 'Twas in me mind he knew I wanted out o' there to go on our picnic."

She laughed and he joined in. His deep laugh rumbled from his chest. She loved the sound and the way his dark eyes sparkled when he was pleased.

When they reached the large boulder, Finn spread the blanket from his bunk. "Although not pretty, 'tis softer than the rock and will protect your skirts."

"I can hardly wait to see what you brought to eat." She opened the basket and set out containers.

"The same is true for me. I asked the hotel's cook to make the basket. She seems a good sort and promised we'd be pleased."

He considered as she opened containers. "Ack, appears this is standard picnic fare."

She handed him a plate heaped with fried chicken, dumplings, pickles, fried squash, boiled eggs, and a biscuit balanced on top. "There's lemonade to drink and bread pudding for dessert. Really, Finn, this is a feast."

"Ah, 'tis glad I am you think so. Truthfully, I'm hungry enough to eat me shoe."

"I'm so glad you thought of this treat." She stretched out her arms above head. "The sun's not too hot, the breeze is gentle, and the sky is clear. What a lovely day for our outing."

After they finished their meal and returned the leftover food to the basket, Finn scooted closer beside her. "And now for the important part o' the afternoon. Me kiss."

She cuddled next to him. "Do you think of nothing but eating and kissing?"

"And what else is there for a couple such as ourselves, I ask?" He pulled her into his embrace.

She met his kiss, parting her lips to receive his tongue. Heat shot through her body, pooling in her private place. When he leaned back, she followed him, to the blanket.

His hand caressed her breast. The nipples tightened and she experienced the need to free them from her dress, but held back. She'd never dreamed she could have such sensations.

They lay on the blanket, half his body above hers. Was this wicked? She should never have let him touch her breasts or responded to his devilish tongue. What would Mama and Papa think if they knew?

"Stella, there's something I've needed to tell you—"

A loud crack interrupted him and the ground gave way. She reached for Finn and he for her, but they were airborne and then falling with the side of the hill. She screamed but the roar of the landslide drowned her voice. And then blackness surrounded her.

Finn came to and fought to focus. He'd been kissing Stella and then the earth gave way. Dirt and rocks covered him. Flexing his body, he climbed up from the debris.

"Stella? Can you hear me? Call out."

She'd been on his right, so he turned and searched. A scrap of green cloth peeked out from the wreckage. He clawed at the rubble trying to reach her.

Onlookers appeared.

"What's happened?" Mr. Frampton asked.

Finn didn't stop heaving rocks out of the way. "Stella Clayton is under here. Help me get her out."

Frampton said, "You'll never get to her with your hands, man. I'll get shovels."

The landslide had stopped only feet from the store's back door. Frampton reappeared with an armful of shovels and passed them out.

"Careful o' her body, men." Finn spotted her shoe and his panic increased. Could she breathe? Had the fall killed her?

While some dug at the piles of dirt, those without shovels heaved rocks out of the way. Council and Lance appeared.

Council knelt beside Finn and started brushing aside dirt. "My Stella! I recognize her dress and foot."

Lance said, "I'll tell Mama and Nettie and be back to help."

Finn glanced up briefly. "One minute we were sittin' on the boulder and the next a loud crack sent us off into thin air. Sounded like an explosion, it did." Finn uncovered her hand.

She didn't respond when he touched her fingers. He almost wept, but he had no time for tears nor to feel for her pulse. Even a few seconds' delay might mean the difference in whether she lived or died. He prayed harder than ever in his life.

Dear Lord, let her be all right. She's a good woman and deserves your loving protection.

His hand touched wool and he pulled at the cloth. "Here's a corner of me blanket we were sittin' on. Pray it softened her fall."

Council had tears on his cheeks. "This is because of the trouble. Instead of me, the bastard took out his wrath on Stella and you."

Sheriff Quinton appeared. "Two more feet and the store would have been hit. Won't say you caused this, but you're always at the scene of trouble, Clayton. You, too, O'Neill."

Without looking up, Finn called, "Check up the hill to see if someone caused the boulder to fall. Sounded like there was an explosion before the land gave way."

The sheriff called by name several miners whose jobs were blasting. "Let's see what we can find."

Finn touched a lock of red hair. "We're getting near her head. Men, keep the shovels away from this area."

Working with their bare hands, Aleski and Piotr joined him and Council. Soon they had Stella freed. She lay covered in thick dust and still as death.

Council clasped her to him. "My baby, Stella, can you speak to me?"

Finn took his handkerchief and brushed her face. He probed her mouth to free anything that blocked her breathing. "Stella, please wake up. Your family and I need you."

He felt at her throat. "Her heart's beating. We must get her to the infirmary. Nurse Williams will know something to help."

Two men rushed forward with a stretcher. "We were summoned to help."

Together, Council and Finn laid Stella on the stretcher. Still she didn't wake.

The men who'd brought the stretcher had come in the ambulance. When Stella was loaded into the wagon, Finn and Council climbed aboard with her. From the distance Mrs. Clayton, Nettie, and Lance ran toward them. Waiting to let them ride would have been polite, but any delay might hinder Stella's life.

The cart's jostling must have been painful to her, but she made no noise. At the infirmary, Finn and Council hopped out and the other two men handled the stretcher.

Inside, Nurse Williams greeted them. "Put her over here. I've set up a screen to give her privacy."

Gently, the men lifted Stella onto the bed.

"Now you men wait by the door. I've got to get her undressed so I can see if she has broken bones."

Mrs. Clayton, Nettie, and Lance rushed in, panting from running.

Obviously out of breath, Stella's mother braced her hand on the doorjamb. "Where is she?"

Council pulled his wife into his arms. "The nurse is checking her."

Nettie weaved around her parents and Finn. "She'll need assistance with sister's clothes. I can help her."

Mrs. Clayton tugged free of her husband. "I can help, too."

Council reached for her. "There's no room, and I need you here, Grace." He buried his face in her hair. "I've never been so frightened, love. She was so still I thought she'd died until Finn found her pulse. I admit I cried like a child."

"Oh, Council, why are these terrible things happening?" She caressed his face before nestling her head against his chest.

Solemn and pale, Lance sat on the floor with his back against the wall.

Seeing people he cared for hurt Finn but not as much as the pain piercing him worrying for Stella. What if she didn't regain consciousness? She'd been buried. Lack of oxygen might have damaged her brain. She might have broken bones.

Only by summoning all his will could he prevent himself from pushing by the screen to see her or curling into a ball on the floor beside Lance. He had to be strong for Stella and her family. By now they seemed like his kin. God willing, one day soon they would be.

The three of them stood for what seemed hours but couldn't have been more than an hour when Nettie rushed toward them. "She opened her eyes."

Finn strode toward the screen and her family followed. When they saw her, she wore an ill-fitting gown and her face and arms had been bathed.

Nurse Williams glared at them. "Did I say you could see her?"

Finn weaved his fingers with Stella's. "No, ma'am, but it she was your family, would you wait by the door?"

"Harrumph, I suppose not. But she has a nasty knot on her head and can't have you all here for long. Five minutes and then you leave."

Mrs. Clayton brushed a hand on her daughter's hair and kissed her forehead. "Finn doesn't have to worry about you being a redhead now. It's dust colored."

Stella presented a weak smile. "Look at my dress."

Mrs. Clayton smoothed a hand along Stella's arm as if making sure she was truly safe. "Who cares about your dress at a time like this? I'll take your clothes with me and get them cleaned up."

Council and Nettie stood at the foot of the bed.

Finn looked into her beautiful blue-green eyes. "Your papa helped dig you out o' the landslide. We were that frantic, I can tell you. Lots o' others helped too."

She looked at each of those gathered around her bed. "I want to go home."

Mrs. Clayton shook her head. "Nurse Williams said you have a concussion. You have to stay here overnight at least."

She frowned "But tomorrow is a school— "

Nettie interrupted. "I can teach both classes for a few days. Lance can help with the young ones. Heavens, sister, you're lucky to be alive. The last of your worries should be school."

Stella closed her eyes, but tears escaped. "Finn and I were having such a nice weekend. Why did this have to happen?"

Finn met Council's gaze. To Stella, he said, "Don't worry about anything. We'll have nicer days ahead. Rest and you'll be wrangling students again in no time."

Nurse Williams reappeared. "Shoo, all of you."

Finn said, "I'd like to sit with her."

"Not a chance, young man. She needs rest and so do you from the looks of you. You come over here and let me check you for damage."

"I'm fine, only dirty." He brushed at his clothes.

"Wait, look at your hands. And yours, Mr. Clayton. Both of you come into my office and I'll clean and bandage them. No arguments now."

Mrs. Clayton nudged her husband forward. "Go on, Council. You must be in pain."

He looked at his bleeding hands. "This is nothing to what my heart feels."

With a grimace, Finn followed the nurse. She was one bossy woman. He'd bet before her hair turned gray, she'd been a redhead.

As they were leaving, they were met by Sheriff Quinton. "Someone tried to blow you to kingdom come, O'Neill. Didn't even hide the evidence."

Council rubbed his forehead. "Who could be behind this, Sheriff?"

"You think I haven't asked myself that question a hundred times? I'm about to lose my job because I haven't found the culprit. Besides that, people have died and others have been injured. We've got to find who's causing these catastrophes. Sorry to say, I need everyone's help."

Finn shook his head and then was sorry. "I've tried to discover who the guilty person or persons could be, Sheriff. So far, I've had no success."

The sheriff removed his hat and ran his hand over his thinning gray hair. "Wasn't Ralph Evans because he's been moved out of town. According to his son, he went to work for Monticello Coal west of here."

Finn "I never thought it was him, Sheriff. Neither he nor his oldest son is smart enough or energetic enough to mange what's been going on here. Whoever is behind the crimes is smart and clever."

The Sheriff hitched up his britches. "Keep your eyes open, men. I'd say both of you are targets of someone."

Finn walked with the Claytons toward their home.

Mrs. Clayton took his arm. "You know you're always welcome at our home, Finn, but for now you need to go to your bunk and lie down. I know it's early, but you're bound to need the rest if you plan to work tomorrow."

"Aye, 'tis right you are. I do feel the need to lie down." He bid them goodbye.

Before he went to his bunk, he sought the storekeeper. "I've lost me blanket. I know 'tis Sunday, but can you sell me another?"

"This once. I'll get you one and put it on your bill, O'Neill. Cold weather's on the way."

He accepted the blanket. "I'm that grateful, Mr. Frampton."

Finn staggered toward the longhouse. While he was working toward Stella, he had high energy. Now, he could barely remain upright.

He met Aleski near the door. "Best get your hands seen to. Piotr too."

Aleski held up his giant paws. "Mine were not so bad. I won't be playing cards for a couple of days, but the others need a break to keep their scrip a few days longer." He laughed, then asked, "How's your woman?"

"She's not mine yet, but she's finally awake. Wants to go home but she has a concussion and will be staying there at least until tomorrow."

"She may not be your wedded wife, but the woman has eyes only for you, O'Neill. You're caught man, same as I was."

"I hope you're right." His surroundings swam by him.

The Pole grabbed Finn's arm. "Hey, don't pass out on me. Here, come along to your bunk."

"Good idea. Me energy left in a rush."

"Come on, get shed of your clothes and lie down. I'll unlace your boots."

When Finn would have protested, the Pole whispered. "I know about the knife and gun, man. I wear the same and spotted the shape."

"Thanks for your help. Guess I'm not as strong as I thought."

"Sure you are. I saw you digging like a machine. You moved more than we move with our picks."

Finn threw off his shirt and kicked out of his britches, remembering to fold the clothes over his boots before he crawled onto his bunk.

The Pole unfolded the new blanket and covered him. "You've a good rest coming."

Finn mumbled another thanks before he burrowed into the pillow and fell asleep.

The next morning, the longhouse dining room was abuzz with talk about the landslide and what caused the boulder's fall.

James sat next to him. "You were dead to the world when I came in. Tell me exactly what happened and how seriously Miss Clayton is injured."

Finn raised his voice so other diners could hear. "Here's what happened." He explained about the picnic and explosion that sent the boulder and them down the hill. "Miss Clayton is in the infirmary. I don't know if she can go home today."

James clapped him on the back. "Sorry I wasn't around to help. I spent the day in Spencer"

Finn frowned. "Didn't know the store there was still accepting scrip."

"They're not, but the good weather made me long to stretch my legs. I remembered the spot where I found you and Lance eating and thought it a good place for my own picnic."

He paused with his fork pointing at James. "Aye, 'twas a lovely day for an outing...until someone blew us halfway to kingdom come."

Talking about the landslide brought back the terror Finn had experienced when he thought he'd lost Stella. He swallowed hard and fought for calm. "I thought sure she was dead from all the debris covering her. If not for me seeing a scrap o' her skirt, reaching her would have taken longer."

James shook his head. "She's lucky then that you spotted her green dress. Are you going to work with your hands bandaged?"

"I've no choice. I'm full of bruises and cuts but I don't want to lose me job."

"Huh, didn't think you liked mining." James forked egg into his mouth.

"I'm here, so I'll do me best. Farland is already that mad at me from the fire. I'll not do anything that gives him cause to fire me."

"Then we'd best get to work." James stood and picked up his plate.

At the mine entrance, Finn met the two men assigned to round out the crew. Both Cesare Garcia and Darby McGee had worked as miners in North Carolina and fell into the job. Finally, Swensen had a chance of getting off the bottom of the board.

As soon as he'd cleaned up after his shift and had supper, he headed to the infirmary. He didn't know if Stella had gone home, but he hoped she'd stay as long as needed. As sore as he was, she must feel worse.

Nurse Williams met him in the foyer. "Here now, where do you think you're headed? Miss Clayton can't have young men parading in and out.

He held up the book he'd brought. "How about if I visit with Mick Gallagher?"

"Much better. He gets lonely." She went back to her office.

Finn ambled into the ward and stopped at Mick's bed. "Here's a book I found near the longhouse. I thought you could read it before I searched for the owner."

The young man checked the title. "Jules Verne. I've heard of him but haven't read this. Reckon people can really go around the world in eighty days?"

"Aye, 'tis possible. Hope you enjoy the book." With a grin at his friend, he put a shushing finger to his lips and stepped around the screen to see Stella.

"Hello, Finn. I was worried because Nurse Williams said she wasn't letting another person come see me. I-I hoped you'd come by when your shift finished."

"You look good. I know you'd rather be at home. Are you in pain?"

She shrugged. "Oh, you know, aches and pains from being thrown and having rocks land on top of me. I'm sure you're sore too. How are your hands?"

He held them out for her to see. "Almost back to normal. Probably heal faster if I could get the grime our o' the crevices."

"Who's doing this, Finn? I'm so worried. Finn if you'd been the one under all the wreckage, I'm not sure I could have reached you in time."

"Others came and 'twas not just me digging. And still we don't know who caused the boulder to fall."

"Mama said the sheriff found explosive evidence."

"Aye, do you not remember a loud bang as the slide began?"

"Sort of, but I thought it was the crack of the rock breaking loose." She clasped her hands. "Finn, I can't help being afraid for you and my family. Someone is determined to disgrace Papa and maybe kill us."

"We can't live in fear or the guilty person wins. I'm that cautious, but I won't stop me routine on account o' some blackguard. He'll be caught soon or I miss me guess. He's getting' cocky and made no attempt to hide the evidence o' explosives he used."

Stella blushed and put her hands on her cheeks. She whispered, "Finn, do you think he was watching us? I mean, we were lying down on the blanket. You touched my breast."

"We did nothing wrong and were both fully clothed. But I suspect he spied on us, the devil. 'Tis how he knew when we were near the edge."

"That makes things worse."

Finn took her hand in his. "Don't be thinking that. I thought you'd be going home today."

She grimaced. "I would have but I made the mistake of letting Nurse Williams know my ankle is sprained. She won't let me go until tomorrow. Honestly, she's like an Army General."

Nurse Williams stepped around the screen. "Aha, I suspected you'd be here with Miss Clayton. Young man, let me see your hands."

Finn held them out to the nurse. "'Tis fine I am."

"Harrumph, well, this Army General," she glanced at Stella, "is ordering you to leave and let Miss Clayton rest."

Resigning himself to the martinet's decree, Finn kissed Stella's forehead. "I'm glad you're better, but stay here until you're really healed enough to leave. I'll find you tomorrow, wherever you are."

Chapter Fifteen

On Wednesday, Finn received a summons to Farland's office. He followed the mousy man whose name he'd never learned. He feared the owner would fire him. Then how would he ever achieve his bargain for Lippincott's ranch?

His feet turned to lead and his body sagged at the thought of being sent home in disgrace. And what would he tell Stella? Hadn't he been that cocky and assured her he'd have his ranch soon?

How could he ask her to leave with him when he wouldn't have more than a single room in someone else's home? Unless he succeeded here, the most he could hope for was managing the former Lippincott ranch instead of owning the fine place. *Almost* accomplishing his dream would be a hard pill to swallow.

When he arrived at the mine's offices, Farland's office door stood open. Finn had no intention of letting the man intimidate him.

He stood tall and rapped on the door facing. "You wanted to see me?"

With a fierce scowl, Farland motioned him inside. "Get in here and close the door behind you."

When Finn had done as requested, Farland yelled, "Instead of finding who's guilty, you continue to be the center of trouble. What have you got to say for yourself?"

What could he say? "I've eliminated people you thought were guilty as well as several I thought might be involved. I admit I haven't found the culprit, but I'm close."

"You have someone in mind?"

He did, but he couldn't prove anything yet. "Not that I can share right now. I need proof and I have none."

Farland stabbed his forefinger at Finn. "I think you're stalling. You have until the 15th`. If you haven't found out who's guilty by then, you're out of here and I'm telling Uncle Vincent you loafed on the job."

Embarrassment turned to anger. "I've not loafed and you know it. I've worked harder than most o' your miners."

"You haven't accomplished what I hired you to do. Remember,

Monday. Now get out of my sight."

Without another word, Finn turned and left. What a sorry excuse for a man Farland was. He walked to the Clayton's home and rapped on the door. Carefully composing his face to hide his anger at Farland, he smiled when Lance opened the door.

"Is Stella home now?"

"Sure, come on in." Lance stood aside to admit Finn. "She's in the parlor and sure being hard to get along with. You know how redheads can be." Lance winked at Finn.

From the parlor, Stella said, "I heard that, Lance Clayton. I'm not too injured to box your ears. Yours, too, Finn O'Neill."

When Finn entered the room, she sat on the bench with her foot propped on one of the kitchen chairs.

Lance danced back and forth out of his sister's reach. "You'd have to catch me first. I can outrun you."

Council grinned and pointed to the ladder-back chair. "Finn, have a seat if you dare."

Finn would have preferred sitting beside Stella, but he figured she needed extra space to adjust her body so she didn't rest on sore places. "You going to stay home from school the rest o' the week?"

"No, I'll be going back to teaching tomorrow. I'm perfectly fine except for a bit of headache and a sore ankle. Already, both are better so I'm sure by tomorrow morning I'll be back to normal."

Mrs. Clayton came into the room. "Now, Stella, a few more days won't hurt."

"Mama, Nettie's exhausted. Even with Lance's help, teaching both classes is too hard when most of her students don't speak English. And if the kids become frustrated, they'll stop coming to school."

Council gave his wife a look filled with love and kindness. "Grace, love, the girl's determined and there's no point arguing. Unless we tie her to a chair or her bed, she'll be going to school tomorrow."

His wife sighed and sat on the kitchen chair that had been moved to the parlor. "I know you're right, dear, but I thought I should try one more time."

Finn asked, "How will you get there, if you're unable to walk."

"I can walk!" She sighed. "Sorry, I snapped at you. Well, I hobble a bit but Nettie will let me lean on her. Nurse Williams loaned me a cane, which helps."

Nettie came into the room. "She turned down the crutch."

Finn recognized the signs and clearly Stella's ire was rising. "I'm sure you'll do well with the cane. And you can whack students with it."

She grinned at him. "I'll only hit wild Irishmen who cause me trouble."

He held up his hands in surrender. "I never cause trouble, although Farland won't agree. He had me in his office again because o' the explosion and landslide. Why he blames me when someone else does these things is beyond me."

Council puffed on his pipe before he spoke. "You're guilty by association with me, I'm afraid. I don't know how long we can last with these horrible events terrorizing us all. He'll likely soon fire me."

"I hope you're safe from attack. Farland's that worried. I figure his profits are way down and he's scared he'll lose the mine."

"He's made a lot of mistakes in dealing with us. His wages are less than he guaranteed. When I asked him about the difference, he said his expenses setting up the mine housing and the associated businesses had been higher than he'd anticipated. Yet he lives in a fine house at the other end of town."

"I've not been there, but 'tis fancy from the outside. I'd wager the man never does without himself." He stood and looked at Stella. "I'll not delay leaving, for I know you need to rest up for tomorrow."

She smiled at him. "You'll come back?"

"Aye, but I'll give you a couple o' days to recover." He bid the family goodbye and went back to the longhouse. He could use some time to recover himself, for didn't his body still feel as if a stampede of horses had run over him?

But he had things to discuss with Stella. The boulder's fall and landslide impressed on him the need to be honest with her. What would she think, though?

Finn waited two days until Thursday and his crew rode down on the rickety platform he hated. "Swensen, I'm asking to leave two and a half hours early today."

The man scowled. "You're my best worker. Is this something important?"

"Aye, I'd not ask otherwise. I'll work all the harder until then."

With a shrug, Swensen agreed. "Don't see how you can work harder than you do, but you have my permission."

He had a pocket watch he'd borrowed from Aleski. At half past three, Finn ascended to the surface. Being alone on the platform, he was able to turn the handle on his own.

Quickly, he cleaned up and changed shirts and britches. Then he walked swiftly to the school a few streets away. Children were already scattering when he arrived. He'd almost cut his appearance too late.

Nettie stood beside Stella's desk. "Hurry, sister. I'm tired and hungry."

Stella looked up and spotted him. "Finn, what a surprise. You didn't get fired, did you?"

"No, I just wanted to talk with you and thought I'd come to the school and see how you're walking."

"Nettie, you go ahead and Finn will walk me home, won't you, Finn?"

He nodded and strode to the desk. "Aye, 'tis why I came. That and a chance to talk to you a while."

Nettie smiled at him. "Okay, then I'll go home. When you're finished 'talking' you can come home. I'm sure Mama will invite you to supper, Finn."

He chuckled at her inference, because the assumption had brought a blush to Stella's lovely face. "We'll not be too long."

Nettie raised an eyebrow. "Uh huh."

Stella hissed, "Nettie?"

Finn held the door for Nettie then closed and locked the door behind her. He went to Nettie's school room and borrowed her desk chair which he set beside at a right angle to Stella's.

A frown marred her lovely brow. "Finn, you have me worried. What's this about?"

"I've been wantin' to talk to you serious like."

She folded her hands on the desk. "I'm listening, but you look so fierce."

"This is a long story, so you please listen to all o' it before you make a judgment. And promise you won't breathe a word o' it until I say 'tis okay. Do I have your word?"

She nodded, her gorgeous blue-green eyes full of questions.

"When I was living with me sister and brother in law, I helped him train horses. He's that gifted and I learned his way o' gentling them. We agreed to go into business together, but I had no money except what he paid me each month."

"But you want your own place, right?"

"Aye, and the large ranch next to Dallas came for sale. The opportunity was too good to pass up. Dallas talked me into going to his grandfather and asking him to loan me the money."

"He's the one the town's named for?"

"The same and he has a lot o' money. But when I got there, Farland was already in Grandpa's study. Grandpa's wife is a harridan, and Farland is her nephew. He wanted me to come here and see if I could learn who's behind all the trouble. If I worked as a miner, he figured I'd have an inside chance the sheriff wouldn't."

She gasped. "You're a spy?"

He held up s hand. "I said hold your judgment, remember? But yes, I've been working undercover to find who's behind this trouble. So far, I haven't had success except to cross off people Farland suspected."

He saw her ire growing. "And one of those was my father, am I right?"

"Aye, but I crossed him off the list right away, for no one works harder or is more fair than he is."

She put her hands at her waist. "But courting me was a way to check on him."

"No, never. I tried to stay away from you so as not to color my opinion o' your father, but I was helpless. I've never experienced such a feeling. From that first evening we met, I couldn't get you out o' me mind."

"But you thought my father was a…a criminal who'd kill the men he worked with every day. How could you cozy up to me when you thought so little of him?"

"I told you I ruled him out right away. I admire the man, but what I think o' you has nothing to do with what I think o' him."

"If you walked with me and went to church with me and picnics and…and, oh my word." She brought her hands to her cheeks. "When I think what we did on the boulder before it fell."

"Stella, love, don't fash yourself about that. I wanted you to know the truth, but I hope you understand that I'm telling you this because I have feelings for you."

"Feelings? You have feelings? What about my feelings, those of my family? You've deceived us all."

"Which is what I'm trying to remedy. Farland's given me until the 15th to find the guilty person or persons." He leaped to his feet and paced. "After that, I'll be gone. I'd planned to ask you to come with me, but if I don't find the blackguard behind the trouble, I'll have naught to offer you except a room at me sister's house."

She stared at him and he couldn't read her thoughts. "Leave my family?"

"Aye, you said you wanted out o' this life. Well, so do I. You can't hate mining more than I do. I've been wracking me brain to think o' something else your papa can do with his talents. I'm sure there're opportunities in McClintock Falls if I but knew o' them."

"You think I'd go with a man who lied to me by omission?"

"That's what undercover means, Stella. Can't you understand I couldn't tell anyone? I shouldn't have told you now. You not knowing doesn't change how I feel toward you."

"Of course it does. How would you feel if you suddenly learned I'm a totally different person that I'd told you?"

Finn reached for her. "I wouldn't care, for I know how I feel about you."

She pulled away. "Just go, Finn. I can get home on my own."

"I won't. If you can't see reason, I'll still walk you home and not bother you again until you invite me."

"No, you won't walk me home." She hobbled toward the coat tree, leaning heavily on the cane. She stumbled and would have fallen if he hadn't caught her.

He grabbed her shawl and put it around her shoulders. "We can go now."

She locked the school behind them. "I'm not changing my mind. Just don't even talk to me."

They walked toward her home.

"Stella, think o' what you're doing. You liked me fine before. I'm the same person."

She stared ahead. "Don't talk to me."

After a block of silence, he tried again. "When you think over what I've told you, you'll see 'twas wrong to be angry."

She whacked his leg with her cane.

"Stella? That hurt."

"Good. Now stop talking."

He waited until they were at her porch. "Remember you promised to keep my secret. I won't bother you again until you invite me." He helped her navigate the steps.

"Goodbye, Mr. O'Neill." She went inside and closed the door in his face.

Defeated, he strode toward the longhouse. Although the thought offered little consolation, at least he hadn't missed supper this time.

Chapter Sixteen

James sat beside him. "What's got you looking so glum?"

"I took off early to meet Stella at her school so I could tell her how I feel about her. Afraid she doesn't want me to call on her again."

On the other side, Aleski nudged him. "Ah, she'll come around. The way she looked at you at the fiesta sent clear signals. The woman is crazy about you."

"Maybe she was. Now she's mad and in no uncertain words told me not to come around."

James gestured with his biscuit. "That's the way of women. They're fickle things."

Finn shook his head. "She's not a thing, James. She's a beautiful and intelligent woman. She just doesn't understand what I tried to tell her."

James used another biscuit to sop up the gravy on his plate. "Tell me and I'll be the judge of whether or not she's right to be angry."

"Not a chance. I'll just give her a few days and hope she comes to her senses."

Aleski nodded approval. "That's the way, Finn. Let her think over what's between you and she'll realize she loves you."

Finn hoped so. He only had a week and then he would have to leave, successful or not. He'd had flirtations, but he'd never felt about a woman the way he did about Stella. She was all he'd dreamed of in a life's companion. She'd be the perfect wife for him.

He pictured her family moving to McClintock Falls. They'd all be together forever. He tossed his plate into the bin by the door and lay down on his bunk. He couldn't concentrate on reading, didn't want to play a game with the other miners.

He wanted Stella. Wanted to hold her and kiss her sweet lips. His heart hurt, as if the organ had truly broken in two.

***

Stella broke into tears as soon as she was inside her home. She didn't want anyone to see her cry, especially Papa. Maybe he wasn't home yet.

Mama rushed at her. "Dear, are you in pain? I thought Finn was coming home with you."

"He walked me home but I sent him away."

"What on earth for? Tell me what's wrong, Stella. Your father will be here in moment and we'll have supper."

"Mama, please, just let me go to my room and lie down. I don't want to be around anyone right now."

Nettie grabbed her arm. "I'll help you, sister."

Once she was in their room, she flung herself on her bed and sobbed. "He lied to me."

"Stella, you know he cares for you. Whatever caused this can be remedied. If you two talk things over you can work this out."

"No, you can't undo a lie. He waited too long to tell me."

"Is he married?"

"No, nothing like that. Please, Nettie, just let me be. I need to be alone. Tell Papa the day tired me out and I need to rest."

"All right. I'll bring your supper on a tray. Shall I light the lamp?"

"Thank you, but the dark suits my mood."

When she was alone, Stella went over every word Finn had spoken today. Then she tried to recall all he'd ever said to her. Remembering all the nice times only made her sink further into depression.

He hadn't cared for her. Oh, she recognized the interest in his eyes, but he was just dallying with her. She'd known he was a dreamer, but she didn't realize how much she'd come to care for him until the explosion and landslide.

She'd envisioned them married and living on a ranch and her family moving nearby. What a fool she'd been. He'd never intended them to be wed. He'd only wanted a means to label her father a criminal.

Recalling she'd asked him point blank if he thought her father guilty, he hadn't said no. His answer was that her father was the hardest worker and best man in Lignite. What kind of reply was that?

Had that been the truth? If so, why hadn't he said "no" outright?

Nettie opened the door and slipped in with her supper. "I told Dad the headache is back and you need quiet and dark. We're all worried about you, sister. Please tell me something."

"I told you he lied to me."

"Stella, I've seen the way he looks at you. He's in love with you. So what has set you against him?"

"I can't tell, only that he lied to me."

"Is he wanted by the law?"

A derisive laugh burst out before she could stop herself. "Quite the opposite. Look, I gave my word I would keep what he told me a secret. Just let me wallow in self-pity tonight and I'll be all right in the morning."

"I'll leave as soon as you've eaten. Mama made you a cup of her headache remedy."

Stella sat up and choked down her meal. She drained the cup and set it back on the tray. "There, are you satisfied?"

"No, but that will have to do. I'll swan, you're harder to reason with than the children at school." She carried the tray and closed the door behind her.

Stella knew Mama and Papa were worried. Probably Lance too. She simply could not face her family tonight. The pain of betrayal was too great.

Somehow, she endured the next two days without breaking into tears. Except at night. Nettie must know she cried, but didn't mention the fact.

On Sunday, she dreaded going to church. Tongues would wag because Finn wasn't with her. Would he attend? He appeared to know all the songs, even said one was his ma's favorite.

She pretended nothing was amiss as she and her family walked to church. Inside, she longed to crawl into a corner and stay.

Ilya Swensen asked, "Where's your young man, Miss Clayton?"

"He isn't *my* young man, just a friend. I suppose he isn't coming today."

"I hope nothing's wrong." Her tone invited sharing a confidence.

"He's probably sleeping late." She pretended to see a friend. "Oh, excuse me. Virginia is signaling me about something."

Nettie whispered, "Virginia? Is that the best you could do? You don't even speak to her."

"She was the first person I saw. Let's sit down so people won't be likely to ask about Finn."

But when Papa and Mama and Lance joined them on the pew, Finn accompanied them. He sat at the other end, by Papa. Dear heavens, what was the crazy Irishman thinking?

Miserable as she was, she couldn't get over her sense of betrayal. When Reverend Mitchell preached on forgiveness, she thought he'd read her mind. Could she forgive Finn?

After the service, Finn shook her father's hand and weaved his way to the exit without speaking to her. She'd been set to snub him, but he hadn't given her a chance. Her anger climbed that he hadn't spoken to her.

But hadn't he said he wouldn't until she invited him? Perhaps he was waiting for her to send him an invitation. She wasn't ready to do that, no matter how much her heart ached.

***

Finn strode out of church quickly as he could before he gave in and went to Stella. Seeing her sitting there all fresh and beautiful tore at him. She should be his fiancée. Darned if he would give up. He'd give her a few days and then he'd try to talk to her again.

In the meantime, he'd keep trying to solve the puzzle of who wanted Council and him dead or looking guilty.

Finn realized there were only two people who fit as the one behind the trouble and he considered both friends. Doing so hurt, but he forced himself to view the facts objectively. This was too important to let his opinions interfere.

Aleski Karpinski was up most of the night and needed cash to get his wife and child to America. He was a nice guy who Finn had worked with on Clayton's crew, but he knew his way around mining. He had supposedly been sick the day the platform cable was cut. He knew about explosives, but he couldn't have been the one following Finn from the Claytons' that night.

James Llewellyn was a friend, but jealous of Finn's friendship with Stella and her family. He often disappeared with no explanation. Did he know how to use explosives? Probably. He'd worked in a mine in Wales before coming to America.

***

Stella dusted off her fingers after erasing the blackboard, happy she didn't have to rely on the cane this week.

Wearing her shawl, Nettie strolled into the room where the older children studied. "I'm ready for home, aren't you?"

She pulled her own shawl around her shoulders. "I'm starving. You'd think I was an orphaned waif on the streets."

Nettie stepped toward the door. "Then let's go."

Both girls jumped when the door opened.

James Llewellyn stepped inside. "Ladies, didn't mean to startle you. Miss Stella, Finn O'Neill had me to stop by and ask you to wait here for him so he can tell you something important. He said even though you're put out with him, please wait here. He said for Miss Nettie to go ahead home, and he'd only keep you a few minutes."

Stella frowned. "Isn't he working for another couple of hours?"

"Not today. He took the day off and went to Spencer on an errand. Well, I'll be on my way. Good day, ladies." James left and closed the door behind him.

Nettie grasped Stella's arm. "Maybe he's going to throw himself on your mercy and propose."

She looked at her sister. "Don't be a silly romantic. I told you I'm not marrying a miner. Not even Finn O'Neill." But her curiosity was aroused. Dared she hope he'd decided to leave Lignite and mining?

Thinking aloud, she said, "I wonder why James was off work early. Never mind, go on Nettie. I have lessons I can work on until Finn arrives. I'm sure he won't be long or he wouldn't have asked me to wait here."

Nettie wavered. "I don't know, sister. Are you sure?"

"If he hasn't shown up soon, I'll follow you and he can come to the house if he has anything to tell me."

With a concerned glance over her shoulder, Nettie pulled her shawl close and left.

Stella hung her wrap on the coat rack and returned to her desk. While she could elaborate her lessons planned for the remainder of the year, she was as fidgety as if covered by ants. She opened a drawer and sorted through the contents.

A slingshot that belonged to Peter Swensen caught her eye. How sad he now worked in the mines at fourteen. True a lot of boys left school at that age, but Peter held promise for a better life. She set the toy weapon aside to return to his family.

The door opened and James Llewellyn returned. This time he held a gun pointed at her. .

"Why do you have a gun? I don't understand."

"You'll understand plenty before the day's over. Stay right where you are." He advanced on her.

She opened her mouth to scream, but he shook his head.

"Yell and you're dead. Here's what's going to happen. You and I are going to go for a walk. Anyone who sees us will think we're cozy, and I'll have this gun against your side. Any attempt to get help and I'll shoot you and whoever you're trying to signal."

"Why are you doing this?"

He tugged her close. "You think your pa will be so full of himself now? And that Irishman will never know what hit him."

"Don't do this." Was James mad or just evil? Focusing on her predicament, she fought for an idea to rescue herself and Finn. None came to her.

They walked through town with his arm around her. She saw a woman she knew but was afraid to try to signal to her. James held the gun against her side and she knew he'd shoot. Praying something would occur to her to distract him, she gazed around for safety.

Finn. James had said Finn wouldn't know what hit him. Dear Merciful Heavens, what did James plan? He had to be the one behind all the disasters. How could he?

He'd been in their home, talked pleasantly to her father. Did he hate him so much? And her? She knew he resented her choosing Finn over him, but the mine incidents had begun far before that happened.

She had to leave a trail. Dragging her injured leg, she hoped she left a trail.

"What are you hanging back for? Pick up your feet and walk."

"You know I hurt my ankle badly when the rock ledge fell. I still have trouble walking and you're hurrying me."

"Don't be casting about for help. I told you I'll shoot anyone who tries to stop us and I mean it." He tugged on her waist.

She repeated, "Why are you doing this? I've done nothing to you."

"Think you're too good for me, don't you?"

"Not at all. No one can explain why he or she feels romantically attracted to one person over another."

"So you're in love with the Irishman as I thought?"

"I-I don't know. I don't know him well enough to say yet. We're just walking out together to get to know one another better."

"You know him as well as you will, for I've plans for him."

"But why?"

"Enough questions."

They left the road and crossed a gravel area to the mine's storage buildings. No, this couldn't be good.

He dragged her past the first two and opened the third. "Get inside and don't be giving me trouble."

When they were inside, he closed the door and shoved her into a corner. After he lit a Davy lamp, he leaned against the wall.

"We'll wait here for your lover." He picked up a coil of rope.

Chapter Seventeen

Finn washed as well as he could without bathing and went in for supper. He couldn't get Stella out of his mind. A dozen times he wanted to confess his love and ask her to wait for him while he sorted out who was guilty. But he couldn't. If she loved him, she'd take him as he was and not accuse him of lying to her.

As soon as he'd eaten, he strode to her house. He'd given her three days to think things through. Maybe she'd reached a decision in his favor. Wanting to see her sweet face and lovely eyes, he tapped on the door.

Lance opened the door and peered around. "Where's Stella?"

Finn stepped inside. "I don't know. I've come to see her."

Nettie rushed toward him. "What do you mean, came to see her? You sent Mr. Llewellyn to tell her to wait at the school for you. We've wondered what on earth could be keeping the two of you so long."

Fear shot through Finn. "I never asked James to tell her anything. I'm going to look for her. Tell your father to get more help. James Lewellyn is the one behind all the trouble."

Finn raced to the school. The door was unlocked and Stella's shawl hung on the coat tree. James had her. Which way would they go?

He stood on the school steps and scanned the area. He found a man's boot print and beside it that of a woman's shoe. Finn strode in that direction, searching for more prints.

Apparently they were walking close together and Finn worried that James had a gun pointed at her. Stella dragged her left foot. Good girl, at least she left more of a trail. But then they turned onto the rocky portion of the road.

Frantic, he scanned each side of the road without success. He stopped to survey the area in the hope of determining which way James had taken Stella. A woman walking along caught his attention.

"Ma'am, did you see a dark-haired man about my size and a red-headed woman walking this way?"

The woman screwed up her face. "If you mean the schoolteacher, she was altogether too snuggled up to the man and right in public. I've a mind to complain to Mr. Farland."

"Which way did they go?"

She pointed. "Toward the storage sheds. Harrumph, I can just imagine what they plan to do there where they'll be alone."

At a run, Finn called, "Please tell that to anyone you see, will you? The man has kidnapped her."

He barely heard her say, "Well, I'll swan."

Which storage building? There were several located beyond the store. As Finn approached, he slowed and scanned the ground for Stella's footprints. Not at the first building.

Moving as silently as possible, he approached the second shed. No prints, so he moved on. At the last building, he spotted the telltale print of a woman's shoe.

He listened with his ear against the shed's thin siding. From inside, he heard the low murmur of voices. Stella's voice. He strained to catch the words.

"James, you're making a mistake. None of us have done anything to you. Why do you hate us so much?"

"You think I want to be stuck in this life? Monticello's owner has offered me enough money to start my own business somewhere. If you'd been friendlier, I might have taken you with me."

"You've killed people, James. How could you murder your friends and coworkers?"

"All necessary to the plan. Monticello wants this mine closed and I aim to make it happen."

"You can't be sure killing Finn and me will accomplish that. Why not put down the gun and let me go?"

As Finn feared, James had a gun. He pulled his small gun from his boot. Not much help unless he was close. Would James let him get within two feet before he fired?

Then he spotted the wire winding toward the second shed. Peering under the building in which Stella was captive, he saw three dynamite sticks. He reached for them, careful not to shake them.

Finn knew nothing about dynamite. He worked the coal while men who specialized in explosives handled blasting. Cautiously, he drew the bundle near. Sweat beaded on his brow as he warily unfastened the wires.

When the fuse was removed, he threw it away from him. Painstakingly, he picked up the dynamite bundle and took it to the next shed. He saw Council and Lance approaching. Aleski must have spotted them because he changed his trajectory to meet theirs. He put his fingers to his lips and pointed at the third shed.

When the men arrived, he whispered the status and told them to stand back because James was sure to fire his gun.

Council said, "I'll storm the shed where Stella's held and you follow."

"No need in making a target o' yourself." Finn showed them his gun.

Aleski grimaced. "Your pea shooter won't help much if he's a revolver. Mine's the same or I'd offer you my gun."

"Whatever he has, there's no point in us all getting shot. Council, you have a family. You do too, Aleski. Lance, stay with your father. I've also a knife in me boot."

Aleski pulled his pepper gun from his boot. "We'll catch him if he escapes the shed."

Reluctantly, Council and Lance agreed to wait behind the second shed. Aleski said he'd open the door for Finn, then run and hit the dirt in the direction opposite Council. That way, they'd have James covered from either direction.

Finn pressed his ear against the wall while Council and Lance reached cover.

James's voice held derision. "Thought you were too good for me, didn't you? But you went stepping out with the Irishman and even let him call you by your first name. This will teach both of you, plus show your uppity father he can't top me."

"I didn't call you by your first name because I didn't want to have a relationship with a miner. I've hated this kind of life. Finn O'Neill plans to buy a ranch someday. Surely you can understand my feelings since you want to escape mining too."

"Why bother talking? 'Bout time your lover got here."

Stella protested, "We're not lovers. We've behaved properly and only held hands and exchanged a few innocent kisses."

"Ha, I saw your 'innocent' kisses at the boulder. Fairly melted the rocks it did."

"You! You were the reason the boulder fell."

"Thought you were supposed to be smart but you're sure slow to catch on. Enough of your pleading and questions."

Finn crept toward the door. He pulled his knife and held it while Aleski opened the shed door and Finn leaped inside. He poised only long enough to throw the knife as James fired.

Pain ripped through his shoulder and he staggered. His knife stuck in James's thigh. Frantic to remove the knife, James lowered his gun. He lunged at James before the other man could fire at Stella.

"Run, Stella!"

She scooted toward the corner. "I'm tied."

James drew the knife from his leg and tossed the blade aside. He raised his gun toward Stella but Finn shot him. In his haste, he missed the man's heart and struck his shoulder. He and James scuffled on the unpainted floor. He gripped the gun James held and succeeded in wrestling it from his hand only to drop the revolver when James tackled him.

"Roll toward the door and outside. Aleski's there."

James gripped Finn's throat. "You'll never live to see her again, Irish."

He couldn't breathe, things around him grew fuzzy. With a giant upward chop to James's arms, he managed to break the strangle hold. His shoulder burned like hell and he hoped James's did too.

Finn kicked James's knife wound. Blood increased to a rapid flow. "Better let me get you help or you'll bleed to death."

James crouched to attack. "Don't think you can trick me, Irish. I'll see you dead before either of us leaves here."

He was ready when James lunged. He swung a hard uppercut to the other man's chin then followed with one to his midsection. When James leaned forward from the impact, he thrust a double-fisted blow on the man's neck.

James went down on his knees, but he reached for the revolver only a foot away. Finn dove for the gun, grasped the weapon, and fired. This shot was true and hit the other man's heart. Surprise spread quickly over James's face before he fell to the floor.

Finn knelt over the man he'd thought of as a friend. Blood pooled under him, mostly belonging to James, but some his own. He felt the other man's neck. No pulse.

He stood and staggered out of the shed. At least a dozen men stood with Council and Lance. They advanced toward the shed.

Stella rushed to throw her arms around him. "Finn, I knew you'd come and I was afraid for your life."

He embraced her. "You'll stain your dress, love."

Tears streamed down her face when she met his gaze. "Do you

think I care? I thought I'd lost you forever. I thought we'd both die."

"That was his plan. Had sticks o' dynamite under the shed."

"He said vile things. I hope I can forget them."

"I doubt you'll forget but mayhap 'twill fade in time. 'Tis not likely we ever will forget this day."

"I've been so foolish. I don't care if you pretend you're a mind reader and run off to join a band of gypsies, I want to be with you forever."

He laughed. If only she knew he'd lived with a band of gypsy-like Irish Travelers. "Stella me love, I've finished me roamin' and will be going to me ranch soon as this mess is straightened. Will you be going with me?"

Her smile radiated love and her beautiful eyes sparkled with tears. "If you'll still have me, nothing would make me happier."

Council extended his hand. "A handshake is little for saving my daughter's life, but perhaps you'll accept the gesture for now."

Finn shook his soon-to-be father in law's hand. With his other, he rubbed at his aching throat. "Sure, and 'tis asking for your daughter's hand I'll be doing." He looked at the woman he loved. "Go with your father and get the stain off that dress. I'll be along when I've talked to Farland and the sheriff."

She held his hand as her father tugged her away. "And the doctor," she called.

"Aye, you bossy red-head." He laughed as he spotted the Lignite sheriff approach.

Aleski said, "I'll stay and back you up, O'Neill. Though I doubt I'm required. Appears word traveled fast."

In the distance, Farland strode rapidly toward them. Finn had a few private suggestions for the mine's owner, but that could wait.

The sheriff's expression left no doubt he was in a foul mood. "What're you involved in now, O'Neill?"

Finn explained about the kidnapping, dynamite, and death. Aleski backed him up as he'd promised.

The man removed his hat and ran his fingers over the gray tufts on his scalp. "You telling me one man, this Llewellyn, was to blame for all the incidents? He must have been twins."

Finn's throat burned like fire from the strangling he'd endured. He croaked when he tried to speak. "I only know what I heard, sheriff. He claimed to want to make Council Clayton look guilty then punish him. Said Monticello Mine's owner recruited him and offered a large sum if Farland's mine went bankrupt."

Farland heard the last sentence. "I knew Monticello was behind this. Didn't I tell you, Thad? With Llewellyn dead, there's no proof." The man let out a string of curses.

"Hold your horses, Wally. I'll search the dead man's gear to see if there're papers that connect them. Man must have had a guarantee of payment unless he's an even bigger fool than he appears."

Aleski interrupted, "If you don't mind, gentlemen, Irish here needs medical attention. He's bleeding like a stuck pig."

Farland appeared to see Finn's wound for the first time. "All right, man, go to the infirmary. The nurse can deal with you until the doctor gets here."

Aleski took Finn's arm. "Appears to me you're wobbling so I'll just go along in case you fall on your face."

By the time they reached the infirmary, he spotted Stella and her sister and mother in the distance, hurrying toward him. He tried to wave, but his arm wouldn't work properly.

Aleski shoved him into the building. "Time for wooing your woman later. You're losing blood like it a faucet."

Finn admitted he was glad to fall across the bed next to Mick. He tried to lift and straighten his legs but hadn't the energy. He closed his eyes. Sounds came as if from far away.

Mick asked, "What happened, Finn?"

Finn heard, but couldn't answer. He flicked a hand toward Aleski.

The Pole adjusted Finn's legs onto the bed. "I'll explain later, Gallagher. For now, this man needs patching."

The nurse hurried in carrying a tray of supplies. "Someone went for the doctor, young man. In the meantime, I've taken care of many a gun wound in my day."

On the side opposite the nurse, Stella laced her fingers with his. He recognized her soft hands and delicate rose scent but couldn't force his eyes open. Apparently her mother helped the nurse for he heard them discussing the wound as they cut away his shirt and union suit. Nettie talked to Mick, explaining what had happened.

Stella leaned in softly and brushed a cool hand across his brow. "I'm here, Finn. You're going to be all right now. Mama and Nurse Williams will fix your wound."

He opened his eyes long enough to see her beautiful face. With a soft exhale, he gave himself over to care and sleep.

When he woke, Stella sat beside him reading. His shirt was gone and bandages swathed his chest. A cloth wrapped his throat.

Stella closed her book and poured a cup of water. She raised his head so he could swallow. "Mama fixed the throat poultice to help take away the soreness. The doctor was here and applied some ointment to your stitches but said Nurse Williams did a fine job removing the lead and sewing up the hole."

"How long did I sleep?"

"You've been here about forty-eight hours."

He wondered if he'd be cheated out of his bonus. "Has Farland been by?"

"Yes, he said come to his office when you're well enough." She reached for his hand. "Finn, I hope you're not angry, but I sent Lance to wire your sister. I know with the new baby and all, she can't come. But if Lance had been wounded so badly, I'd want to know."

"Might send someone else to fetch me. When I know more, I'll write her."

"I'm glad you're not angry. I-I know I didn't have a right, but I thought how I'd feel if I were in her shoes."

"You're a good woman. Glad you're my woman and I'm your man."

She leaned over and kissed him.

A deep voice said, "Looks cozy."

Stella jumped as if a kid caught stealing candy.

He laughed. "Josh, you sure got here fast." He turned to Stella. "This rogue is Josh McClintock, Dallas's rascal cousin that's more like his brother. Josh, this beautiful woman is Miss Stella Clayton, my fiancée. See you remember I've already spoken for her."

Josh removed his Stetson. "The author of the wire. Cenora said to tell you she sure appreciates you letting her know her big brother's hurt. Not sure I appreciate being sent here, but gave me a chance to travel a little."

"Haven't you been over this country before?" Finn asked.

"Nearby but never been to Lignite. Not much to look at, is the place?"

Stella giggled. "You should have to live here."

Josh pretended to be horror stricken. "No, thanks. Say, Finn, they have a hotel here? I have orders to make sure you're walking around before I return. I'm supposed to bring you back, but I suspect you'll be delayed on account of your fiancée being so pretty."

Used to Josh's flirting, Finn didn't bother to comment on the calf-eyed stares Josh sent Stella's direction. "There's a hotel up the hill by the mine office."

Finn glanced at Stella before answering. "I don't plan on being delayed long. Stella's willing to return with me to McClintock Falls."

Stella nodded. "The sooner the better."

Nettie came in and stopped when she saw Josh. Her blue eyes widened. "Sister, I came so you could go home to supper."

Finn made introductions.

Josh's eyes lit with interest. "Another gorgeous Clayton woman. I swear your parents must have a corner on the market."

Nettie stared as if unable to speak. She blushed and came to stand beside her sister.

Stella rose. "Mr. McClintock, if you'd care to accompany me, you're welcome to eat supper with my family. Simple fare, probably stew, but Mama's a good cook."

"I'd be pleased, Miss Clayton. Please, since we're going to be family, call me Josh." After a gallant bow, he offered his arm.

She sent Finn a parting smile. "I'll see you later, Finn."

Nettie stared after them as if in a trance.

"Have a seat, Nettie. Don't let Josh turn your head. He's not the sort to settle down. More like wooing every single woman in the state."

"He's very handsome, but I recognize the type. He'd never be seriously interested in me."

Finn shook his head. "Quite the contrary, he will be. I spotted the interest. Why I'm warning you is that he never *stays* interested. He flits from woman to woman like a butterfly in a flower garden. He's not mean-spirited. Though he's old enough, he hasn't grown up yet."

"I see. Thanks for saying he'd be interested in me, Finn. That was kind of you."

"I wasn't being kind, Nettie. I hope to save you a broken heart. Josh is the love-them-and-leave-them type and that's not you. You're the strong, one-man woman type who'll make some man a great husband."

"Thank you again, Finn. That's a very nice comment. I'm glad Stella and you are going to be married."

Chapter Eighteen

Finn was able to leave the infirmary two days later.

With Stella beside him, he walked to Farland's office. "I hope he doesn't welsh on our deal. Or try to pay my bonus in scrip."

"Do you have paperwork?"

"No, but Grandpa McClintock heard him promise."

She gave his arm a squeeze. "We'll manage no matter what Mr. Farland does. You can always go back to work for your brother in law, can't you?"

"Sure, but…well, here we are. I'll save other news for later."

Josh had stopped by and told him Grandpa had the ranch all ready for him. Most of Lippincott's hands were remaining. Lippincott left a few pieces of furniture that didn't fit in the house in town. Grandpa had even negotiated two hundred head of cattle. With news like that, how could he not feel good as new?

He longed to be there with Stella by his side to walk through the house, the barns, and ride across the land. And he set Josh to thinking on a job for Council that would get him out of mining. Rather than build false hopes, he decided to wait until the deal was sealed before he mentioned details to Stella.

She waited in an outer office while Finn went in to speak to Farland.

The man stood when he walked in. "Have a seat, O'Neill. Can't tell you how happy I am to have this ordeal behind me." He sat on his office chair.

Finn took the chair indicated. "I'll be going back to McClintock Falls now, Mr. Farland. I came for my bonus."

"Sure, sure. Let's see now, what did I say that would be?" He searched through papers on his desk.

"You guaranteed me double the salary so I'd have a down payment for me ranch."

"So I did, so I did. Of course, your salary's been in scrip."

"Don't try to push off scrip on me for the bonus. Your uncle heard you agree to the terms and I'm holding you to them."

"You act as if I'd cheat you. Let's see," He jotted on a scrap of paper. Pulling out his checkbook, he wrote a draft.

Finn looked at the amount. Anger boiled in him. "You have tried to cheat me, Farland."

"I gave you the same exchange I gave Mr. Karpinski. That's only fair."

"No, you weren't fair to him or to any o' your employees. Let me tell you what's fair. You're going to lower the charges in your store to what it costs you to provide them. You'll build a library and a better equipped school that offers adults a chance to learn to read and write also and you'll hire qualified teachers for I think the Clayton sisters will no longer work for free."

"Ridiculous. I can't afford those things."

"Aye, you can and you'll give all the workers a ten percent raise. You'll do that to keep out the unions. Were the unions to come in, you'd spend far more than what I've outlined."

"Damned if I won't fire that troublemaker Hartford for talking up unions."

"Oh, no, you may think firing Hartford will keep out unions, but you're that wrong, man. You think he's the only one wanting a union? The working conditions in this mine beg for the unions to step in. Then you'll have strikes and inspections. You'll have ten times the headache James Llewellyn caused."

Farland's jaw set and his expression as petulant as a misbehaving child's. "I don't want unions in here. They're nothing but trouble."

"You bet they will be if they see this place." Finn shoved the draft at Farland. "I'll have you double this amount on a fresh draft. Else I'll tell everyone I know to ask for a union representative to come here."

Farland paled. "You wouldn't dare? Why, we're almost related."

"Then don't try to cheat me."

Face red, Farland opened his checkbook and penned another draft. "Take this and be damned."

Finn glanced to make sure the amount was correct this time. "I'd say workin' here has been a pleasure, but t'would be a lie."

He strode from the office and offered his arm to his intended. "Shall we go, love?"

She smiled up at him. "I'd be delighted." Finn patted her slender hand where it rested on his arm. "Love, I've already spoken to your father and he gave us his blessing. Now we need to discuss our wedding."

She sent him a perplexed gaze as they walked down the hill toward her home. "When did you speak to Papa?"

"Remember when you wouldn't talk to me but I came to church and sat by? I'd asked Council on the way into the service."

"But, Finn, how did you know I'd change my mind?"

He grinned at her. "Did I not say we're soul mates? All I knew is I couldn't live without you. I would have pestered you until you either shot me or promised to marry me."

She returned his smile. "And you remember that Papa doesn't own a gun, right?"

He couldn't stop the laugh bubbling up from inside him. "Aye, but 'tis a resourceful woman you are. I'm sure you could have found one."

"Can we be married here or do you want to be married in McClintock Falls?"

"Let's marry here and soon. Josh said there's a house not that far from the ranch being saved for your family. About halfway between the ranch and town. I remember the place, and 'tis far nicer than any have here except Farland's."

"How will my parents live? Are there jobs available?"

"Yes, here's your house. Let's wait until we're inside and we can talk to your folks."

Inside the house, her mother and siblings rushed at them. Josh sat in Council's chair where, no doubt, he'd been flirting with Nettie.

Stella still held his arm. "There's so much to tell, but we need to plan the wedding."

"Your father will be here soon. He quit his job."

Stella clapped her hands together and ran toward her mother. "Mama? When did he do that?"

"While Finn was in the hospital. Papa said if you were moving to McClintock Falls, so were we. That's all he'd been waiting for and why we've saved his bonuses."

Grace came and placed her hand on Finn's arm and gazed at him with tears gathering in her eyes. "Josh tells us you'd asked about a job for Council and that there's a house for us there. How can we ever thank you?"

Finn slid an arm around Stella and smiled at her mother. "You've treated me so kindly that I've felt a kinship since we met. By letting me marry your daughter, you'll truly become my family."

Grace hugged Stella then gazed at each of her children. "We couldn't tell you for fear our dreams would be impossible. The reason your father took this job was to get us to America where he could start over when his contract was finished."

Stella put her hands on her cheeks. "Oh, I'm so embarrassed for all those times I fussed at him to change jobs. Poor Papa."

Nettie grabbed Lance's hands and danced around the room.

Lance asked, "When do we leave?"

Their mother smiled at her children. "I suppose right after the wedding."

Stella grabbed her mother's arm. "Mama, what am I to do? My best dress is ruined. Will you let me wear your wedding dress?"

Grace clapped her hands together. "Why do you think I've saved it all these years if not for you girls? Of course the styles have changed and there's no bustle but the dress is real silk and the finest I've ever owned."

Lance rolled his eyes. "If this is all you're going to talk about, I'm going in the other room."

Council must have heard as he came in the door. "We've plenty to talk about. Only a few more days to get packed and vacate the premises." He shook Finn's hand. "Glad to see you up and about."

Finn guided Stella toward her mother and sister. "Stella, I agree with whatever you ladies arrange for the wedding as long as the date is soon. Your father, Josh, Lance, and I have plans to make for the move."

Stella took her mother by the hand and guided her toward the bedroom. "Let's see your dress, Mama. And we have to decide what you and Nettie will wear."

Council sat on the ladderback chair. "I can't tell you how free I feel to be leaving, yet at the same time trembling with terror over the prospect of having quit my job."

Finn sat on the bench. "Did Farland give you trouble over leaving?"

"I'd fulfilled my year here, which was the agreement I signed to get transportation from England. Farland was rude as is his way. When I told him he had better treat his men more fairly or he'd be seeing unions move in, the man turned so red I thought he would have an apoplectic fit. I spoke the truth though."

"Aye, 'tis the same thing I told him. Now, tell us what we need to do to get you ready to leave."

Josh reared back. "Us?"

Finn nodded. "Will you not be my best man?"

"I joked, for I'd planned to help these fine folks move out of this awful town. Grandpa owns that little row of three houses on the way to town from the ranch. The center one has just become vacant."

Council asked, "Does the house include furniture?"

Josh stood and stretched. "Doesn't come furnished, but I wired Mama to find enough for your family. Gran changes up her house every few months, or so it seems. There'll be plenty stored somewhere."

Lance perked up. "Will I have my own room?"

Finn nudged his soon to be brother-in-law. "Aye, 'tis a nice house and much improved over this one. You'll have more room and better furnishings."

Council surveyed the room as if mentally taking stock of things to pack. "I spoke to Frampton at the store and he's given me crates for our things. He'd only burn them so I didn't mind asking. I'll walk to Spencer and rent a wagon to get the crates out of Lignite. What I'll do then is open to question for I've no idea where McClintock Falls is or how to get there. And this time of year, the weather is unpredictable."

Josh looked at Finn before speaking, "Texas weather is always unpredictable, but all you have to do is get your things to the station and loaded on a train. At Sabinal, we get off and wait for my folks to arrive with a couple of wagons. There's a hotel there if the train gets in late. Otherwise, we can load up and head for home."

Finn wanted to jump with excitement. "I can hardly wait." He spoke to Council and Lance. "After mining towns, you'll love McClintock Falls."

Josh paced the small room. "I've invited that kid, Gallagher, to come too. He's about Daniel's age and I figure Mama will find a place for him until he's healed. The trip will be rough, but he's eager to go with us."

Surprise filled Finn. Josh was a good man and hard worker, but he didn't usually think of others. "That's real nice of you, Josh. His family's dead and he has no one."

"So he told Lance. Can't stand seeing a fellow laid up and alone. I know Mrs. Clayton and Lance visited him, but they'll be gone soon. He needs to be in a home with good food and care." Josh reached for his hat. "I'll head on to the hotel and make sure arrangements are on schedule there for whenever the women set the wedding date. I'll be here early tomorrow to help pack your belongings."

After Josh had gone, Finn stood. "Reckon I'd better go, too. I'll be here in the morning and help pack and hopefully get married."

"I'll send Stella out to tell you goodbye." Council stood.

Finn held up his hand. "I'm sure they're busy with plans. Just tell her I'll bring my best clothes, but you know they're not good. I don't have fancy things, but what few I have are back at home."

"I'll see if Ulys has anything you can wear. He's about your size."

"Thanks. Goodnight."

***

The next day, Stella would have sworn a thousand gnats attacked. She could hardly stay still. Events were moving so quickly. Suddenly, all the things she'd dreamed were within reach. She longed for Finn to appear and share in the wedding plans she and her mother and sister had made. He'd been by early but Mama insisted he not see her. He and Lance had left to go rent a wagon and team.

Papa came in the door wiping his feet. "I spoke to the minister. Reverend Mackenzie is coming to the hotel lobby at half past six. You have reservations at the hotel for tonight. Josh is hosting a wedding supper in the hotel dining room. But now he's gone with Finn and Lance."

She clasped her hands to her breast. "A real wedding supper at the hotel? That's wonderful, Papa."

"Indeed, and will cost more than I make in a month. Generous of him but he insisted. Said you could invite friends if you wish. Thought I'd invite my crew if you don't mind."

"By all means." She and Nettie had no special friends she wished to invite. The thought saddened her. She and Nettie worked together and relaxed at home with family. Other women in town their ages were married with small children.

Papa fed coal into the stove. "All my wedding-related tasks are done so I'll start crating up things in the bedrooms."

Stella hurried after him "Don't pack the things I'll need for the wedding and tonight or for the trip. I put everything except the wedding dress in the large valise on the bed."

Mama turned her around and guided her into the kitchen. "Nettie and I have packed everything we'll need for the trip. Our wedding clothes are hanging on pegs. Papa won't pack anything we'll use before we leave. I'd better cook up some things for breakfast and our trip so we can pack the staples."

"I'll help, Mama. I'm so excited I'll explode if I don't keep busy. Why don't you supervise Papa and send Nettie in to help me."

***

Finn smiled as if he'd been made king. He looked around the room where he and his bride would spend their last night in Lignite. Where Stella and he would make sweet love. Tomorrow they'd leave for the fine ranch he'd purchased. Aye, he knew Grandpa held the mortgage for the coming fifteen years, but he considered the place his and Stella's.

Before he knew where the day had gone, 'twas time to go downstairs for the wedding. He adjusted his tie once more and shrugged into the jacket that almost fit. Still, 'twas kind of Ulys to loan his only suit.

Butterflies in his stomach threatened to carry him away as he descended the stairs. As he stepped from the last stair tread, Reverend Mackenzie walked into the lobby.

"Looks like you're ready to wed, young man. Is the bride here yet?"

"No, sir, but I see guests have already arrived." Finn gestured toward where chairs had been set up in a room off the lobby. "Shall we join them?"

Josh stood pacing. "Glad you're here. I have the ring and Mrs. Clayton sent this greenery for your lapel."

Finn smiled at the other man's nervousness. Any talk of a wedding usually sent Josh running. He spotted the men from Council's crew and shook each man's hand. "Thanks for coming."

He took Aleski aside. "When your wife and boy get here, come to McClintock Falls. There'll be a house and job for you there." He nodded toward Pakulski and Bosko. "For your kin too. They're building a new courthouse and need stone masons. But it's a growing town and you could get work as carpenters or shop keepers or on a ranch."

"I've no way to contact Reina until she gets here. As soon as she arrives, I'll on my way out of here and show up on your doorstep."

"I'll look forward to that day."

He stopped and told Jose and Maria the same thing. Jose had to think over the offer. "Farland, he announced changes. I am happy to have a house and a raise. He say maybe soon I'll be made a crew chief."

"Do whatever makes you happy. The offer is always open."

"Sorry to interrupt. Your bride arrived." Josh hurried him to the front of the room by a podium.

He, Josh, and the minister took their places. Smiling to himself, he wished he could have seen Stella's face when she saw that he'd rented a covered carriage for her trip to the hotel and tomorrow to the train.

Lance ushered his mother and seated her in the front row reserved for her and Council. Nettie walked toward them wearing her blue dress. Her golden hair was in an intricate hairdo atop her head with the blue ribbon he'd given her woven among the curls.

He almost collapsed when he saw Stella. She'd told him the dress was gray silk trimmed with ruches, whatever those were, of the same material and matching satin ribbon. All he knew was she looked like a queen deigning to mingle with the peasants. Her lovely hair was piled high with a long, thick curl dangling down in front of her right shoulder. Around her throat, she wore a locket.

How could someone so beautiful and perfect be marrying a wild Irish boy like him? Humbled and honored, he couldn't speak, couldn't breathe, couldn't move. Somehow he took her hand from her father.

He must have answered the minister's cues for soon they were pronounced husband and wife.

Reverend Mackenzie said, "Friends, I present Mr. and Mrs. Finn O'Neill."

Applause and cheers broke out.

Stella clung to him and he realized she was as nervous as he was. Her smile was wide and her lovely eyes sparkled with happiness. He kept his arm around her for he thought they could support one another.

Nettie hugged her sister, then Finn.

Grace Clayton did the same thing. "Now you must call me Mama and call Council Papa. You're our son, and we couldn't be happier."

Council draped an arm around his shoulders. "That's the truth, son."

Josh raised his hands for silence. "You're all to be my guests at the wedding supper. They're ready for us in the dining room."

Finn cupped his bride's elbow and escorted her to the head table. When he'd seated Stella, he leaned toward Josh. "What a grand feast you've arranged. Man, are you made o' money?"

"Mama and Cenora ordered me to arrange this. Papa and Dallas are splitting the cost with me, so don't feel guilty. They've been sending wires for over two days."

"Still, you've my thanks. I could never have afforded anything like this nor could Council."

Josh flashed his roguish smile. "As long as it's for someone else's wedding, I don't mind."

He seated Nettie while Council seated Grace. Lance joined his parents.

When everyone had been served, Josh rose and tapped on his glass. "The first time I met Finn, he had my cousin Dallas captive. Well, not exactly captive, but Dallas had wed Finn's sister. I guess you'd say she had him captive."

Josh paused for the laughter to quiet. "She still does, for they're much in love and just welcomed their first child. I'm proud to call Finn O'Neill cousin and now happy to add the Claytons as kin," he glanced down at Nettie, "especially the pretty ones."

Nettie blushed.

Everyone laughed.

Stella leaned toward Finn. "Did he catch the art of blarney from you?"

He whispered, "Comes by it naturally."

Josh raised his glass. "To the bride and groom."

Finn raised his glass and gazed at his beautiful bride. "To us, my love."

Chapter Nineteen

McClintock Falls, Texas

Stella gasped as they crested a rise and Finn stopped the wagon and set the brake. "This is ours? All of this?"

He slid his arm around her shoulders. "Same as. Remember, I have fifteen years to pay off Grandpa McClintock. Means a lot o' work, but I know I can succeed with you by my side."

Holding on to one another, they sat taking in the view. The southwesterly breeze carried a chill, but the bright sun overhead warmed them. The large two-story home appeared to have been added on to over the years. Painted bright white, black trim shined in the morning light. Heavens, how would she ever fill such a place with their few belongings?

The main barn was as tall as the house. In back of the home in which she and Finn would live stood a couple of small houses and what she thought was a bunkhouse. A large windmill was between their house and the two smaller ones. The beautiful scene stole her breath and she fought joyous tears threatening to spill.

She placed a hand at her chest, wanting not only to savor this moment but to store this minute in memory forever. "Finn, I never dreamed I'd ever live in such a grand place. I thought there'd be a house the size of the one my family lived in at Lignite and a barn and chicken pen. There are so many buildings the ranch is almost a small town."

"Aye, 'twould appear so, but every building has a purpose. I see our cowboys are hard at work, Soon I'll have me own hands full keepin' up with them." He appeared as awestruck as she was.

She wanted to reassure him he didn't face alone all the work in store. "Your sister told me I need to gather the eggs each morning and feed the chickens. She showed me the schedule Kathryn set up to help her. I copied everything so I can be a good ranch wife."

Sending her a look filled with love, he brushed her hair from her face. "Of course you'll be a good wife, my love. You only have to be by my side to achieve that. I'll do me best to be the husband you deserve." He planted a gentle kiss on her lips.

After releasing the break, they drove up a tree lined drive to the front hitching rail. The closer they came, the better the house appeared. When Finn set the break and climbed down, she was too excited to wait for him to come around to help her. She made her way to the ground.

One of the cowboys came running. "I'll take care of the wagon and horses."

Finn "I'm obliged."

They joined hands and walked up the front walk. Stella couldn't believe the changes in her life in the past few weeks. They threatened to overwhelm her.

She glanced at the wedding ring Finn had placed on her finger two weeks ago. He fairly danced up the steps, tugging her along. Not that she minded.

Obviously, Finn was not as confident as he tried to appear, for his hands trembled when he inserted the key into the lock. Her pulse raced with excitement and she had difficulty not jumping for joy. He pushed open the door then swept Stella into his arms and carried her over the threshold.

Emotion choked his voice. "Here we are, my love, in our own home." He set her down and they both surveyed the foyer.

She stared at the staircase that wound upward. "I can't believe this is ours. It's beautiful and so large."

"For a family. But I'm having trouble taking this all in, too." He planted a kiss on her lips.

She broke the kiss to whirl across the floor. "Let's explore our home before we devote ourselves to one another."

Hand on his heart and his dark eyes dancing, he said, "You wound me. 'Tis second place to a house I am."

She laughed but waited for him to reach her. "You know that's not true. I simply can't believe all the wonderful things that have happened to us."

"Me, either. I dreamed o' this ranch, but it wouldn't be a home without you here with me. And now your folks will be nearby."

"Thank heavens for that. Papa will live longer now that he's out of the mines. Mama's so happy with the house Mr. McClintock rented to them, which is the nicest place they've ever lived."

The Lippincott's had left what furniture didn't fit into their smaller house in town. A sideboard took up the end of the dining room near a table that would easily accommodate twelve. She pictured both their families here for Christmas or other holidays.

In the parlor, a lumpy sofa and well-used chair facing the fireplace at least gave them somewhere to sit. Thank goodness, draperies were on the windows in both rooms. At least the cowboys couldn't see in the windows.

In the kitchen she hurried to the stove. "Would you look at this range? I can cook huge meals. Am I supposed to cook for the cowboys?"

"No, love, there's a cook in the bunkhouse where they eat."

"I wonder why she didn't take her washtubs?" Stella stared at two large tubs stored in the screened-in porch.

"There's a laundry in town where a lot o' ladies have their wash done. Not Ma, but she told me about the ladies who work there."

"Oh, there's another wing of rooms here." She tugged him with her and into the next room.

His face clouded with worry as he peered at the shelves of ledgers. "This was Lippincott's office. I hope you'll help me keep the ranch records, love."

She knew he agonized because she had more schooling than he. "I'd love to. Then we'll truly be partners. Let's see what's next."

A small sitting room or back parlor looked out onto the garden and delighted her. "I'll bet this is where they spent most of their time, don't you?"

"I'd say so. Nice view o' the flowers and looks like a vegetable patch."

She clasped her hands to her breast. "We'll grow most of our food. That's wonderful. We'll be independent."

He slid his arm around her waist. "Yeah? What about those cowboys who work for us?"

Laughing, she whirled and grabbed his arm. "Come on, let's see upstairs. Oh, I hope they left us a bed."

He wiggled his eyebrows and pretended to leer at her. "Not any more than I do."

She ran her fingers over the beautiful wood banister as they climbed the steps. Would their children slide down this someday? Would they be boys or girls, have red hair or dark brown, have blue eyes or brown?

Upstairs, there were five rooms. The first four were equally nice-sized bedrooms, each with a small fireplace and room for a chair and table in addition to the bedroom furniture they'd have eventually. Additional furniture might be a long time coming. The fifth room offered a great surprise.

She turned slowly, taking in every corner. "This bedroom is big enough for a house. Half of our cottage at Lignite would fit inside this."

"Bigger than the cottage where I was born and the caravan where Mac and Vourneen live. I'll bet they had a sofa and chair up here near the fireplace. Best o' all, they left a bed, though I'd wager it isn't the one they used." He pushed to test the mattress.

She barely glanced at the iron bedstead while she focused on each part of the room. "Who cares? We have a place to sleep tonight."

"And to use now." He pulled her into his arms and gently laid her on the mattress then climbed beside her.

She slid her arms around his neck and pulled him to her. "Mister O'Neill, I am the luckiest woman alive."

He spread her glorious red hair around her. "And I'm the luckiest man ever on this earth, my love. The world belongs to us."

She allowed the euphoria inside her to burst forth. "And we belong with each other, my soul mate. Forever."

If you'd like to know about my new releases, contests, giveaways, and other events, please sign up for my newsletter here.

Thank you for reading my book. If you enjoyed this story, please leave a review wherever you purchased the book. You'll be helping me and I'll appreciate your effort—so will prospective readers.

CAROLINE CLEMMONS

Read Caroline's Amazon bestselling western historical titles:

The Most Unsuitable Wife, Kincaids book one

The Most Unsuitable Husband, Kincaids book two

The Most Unsuitable Courtship, Kincaids book three

Gabe Kincaid, Kincaids book four

Brazos Bride, Men of Stone Mountain book one
Buy the Audiobook here

High Stakes Bride, Men of Stone Mountain book two
Buy the Audiobook here

Bluebonnet Bride, Men of Stone Mountain book three

Tabitha's Journey, a Stone Mountain mail-order bride novella

The Texan's Irish Bride, McClintocks book one

Save Your Heart For Me, a western adventure novella

Happy Is The Bride, a sweet humorous wedding novella

Long Way Home, a sweet Civil War adventure novella

Caroline's Time Travel

Out Of The Blue, 1845 Irish lass comes forward to today

Caroline's Contemporary Titles

Be My Guest, mildly sensual

Snowfires, sensual

Home Sweet Texas Home, Texas Home book one (sweet)

Caroline's Mysteries:

O'NEILL'S TEXAS BRIDE

Almost Home, a Link Dixon mystery

Death in the Garden, a Heather Cameron cozy mystery

Take Advantage of Bargain Boxed Sets:

Wild Western Women, five western historical novellas by USA Today bestselling authors Kirsten Osbourne and Callie Hutton, and Amazon bestselling authors Sylvia McDaniel, Merry Farmer, and Caroline Clemmons, plus short stories by Merry Farmer and Caroline Clemmons

Mail-Order Tangle, a western historical duet includes Mail-Order Promise by Caroline Clemmons and Mail-Order Ruckus by Jacquie Rogers

Hearts and Flowers: Save Your Heart For Me, Happy Is The Bride, Long Way Home

10 Timeless Heroes, time travels include Out Of The Blue and novels by Sky Purington, Skhye Moncreif, Donna Michaels, Beth Trissel, P. L. Parker, L. L. Muir, Linda LaRoque, and Nancy Lee Badger

Rawhide n' Roses 2,000 word short stories by fifteen western authors introduce readers to their voice and style

CAROLINE CLEMMONS

About the Author

Caroline Clemmons is an Amazon bestselling author of historical and contemporary western romances whose books have garnered numerous awards. Her latest release is O'Neill's Texas Bride, book two of her popular McClintock series. A frequent speaker at conferences and seminars, she has taught workshops on characterization, point of view, and layering a novel.

Caroline is a member of Romance Writers of America, Yellow Rose Romance Writers, From The Heart Romance Writers, and Hearts Through History Romance Writers. Her latest publications include the acclaimed historical Men of Stone Mountain series: BRAZOS BRIDE, HIGH STAKES BRIDE, and BLUEBONNET BRIDE and the audio books of BRAZOS BRIDE and HIGH STAKES BRIDE.

Caroline and her husband live in the heart of Texas cowboy country with their menagerie of rescued pets. Prior to writing full time, her jobs included stay-at-home mom (her favorite), secretary, newspaper reporter and featured columnist, assistant to the managing editor of a psychology journal, bookkeeper for the local tax assessor and—for a short and fun time—an antique dealer. When she's not indulging her passion for writing, Caroline enjoys reading, travel, antiquing, genealogy, oil painting, and getting together with friends. Find her on her blog, website, Facebook, Twitter, Goodreads, and Pinterest.